Buffalo and Beaver

by the same author

THE BLACK BUCCANEER
DOWN THE BIG RIVER
LONGSHANKS
RED HORSE HILL
AWAY TO SEA
KING OF THE HILLS
LUMBERJACK
THE WILL TO WIN AND OTHER STORIES
WHO RIDES IN THE DARK?
T-MODEL TOMMY
BAT: THE STORY OF A BULL TERRIER
BOY WITH A PACK
CLEAR FOR ACTION!
BLUEBERRY MOUNTAIN
SHADOW IN THE PINES
THE SEA SNAKE
THE LONG TRAINS ROLL
SKIPPY'S FAMILY
JONATHAN GOES WEST
BEHIND THE RANGES
RIVER OF THE WOLVES
CEDAR'S BOY
WHALER 'ROUND THE HORN
BULLDOZER
THE FISH HAWK'S NEST
SPARKPLUG OF THE HORNETS
THE BUCKBOARD STRANGER
GUNS FOR THE SARATOGA
SABRE PILOT
EVERGLADES ADVENTURE
THE COMMODORE'S CUP
THE VOYAGE OF THE JAVELIN
WILD PONY ISLAND

Buffalo and Beaver

by Stephen W. Meader

Illustrated by Charles Beck

ISBN 978-1-931177-18-4 cloth
ISBN 978-1-931177-19-1 paperback

SOUTHERN SKIES

LITTLE ROCK, ARKANSAS

www.southernskies.com

Dedication

The republication of this book is dedicated with love to Dr. James Yee Suen by his best friend, Jerry Atchley.

Foreword

In the early days of the West—long before the arrival of cowboys or cavalry, six-shooters or wagon trains—there were the Mountain Men. Alone, or in little groups of two or three, they crossed the Great Plains, followed the rivers to their sources, explored the vast, unknown wilderness of the Rockies. They went where no white men had ever been before.

Through cold and snow they wintered in the high valleys and packed out their furs in the spring, for fur was their business. They found the beaver in countless thousands and trapped them for their skins. When deer and buffalo were abundant, they had meat. Otherwise, they pulled their belts tight and went hungry. Hostile Indians, too, were plentiful. It took brave, resourceful men to survive in that country.

They were a restless breed, always pushing on to find fresh hunting grounds beyond the next white mountain range. Some of them had the vision to appreciate the lonely grandeur of what they saw. Perhaps it was that, even more than the quest for fur, that brought them back year after year to endure new hardships.

These were the men who discovered the passes and blazed the trails across the mountains. To them we owe the swift expansion of our land from ocean to ocean.

This story takes place in the 1820's, the heyday of the Mountain Men. Some of the characters are historically true. Others, like young Jeff Barlow, his father, and Wind River Slim, are fictional, though I have tried to make them true to type. For those who would like to read more about this exciting period, I would recommend such splendid books as *The Long Rifle* by Stewart Edward White and *The Big Sky* by A. B. Guthrie, Jr.

Stephen W. Meader

chapter 1

Jeff came up from the field at suppertime, carrying the hoe on his bare, brown shoulder. Hoeing corn was a chore he hated—especially the first or second hoeing, when the blades were hardly bigger than the weeds. If the hoe slipped and he dug up a hill of corn, he knew Uncle Wash would purse his lips and shake his head and look black as a thundercloud. There wouldn't be any licking—just silent disapproval that made him feel mean and small.

It was the end of May, and the summer heat had come full blast. Even now, in the shade of the two tall buckeye trees that overhung the farmhouse, Jeff could feel the sweat streaming on his bare chest and arms. He flung down the hoe by the hollowed split log that served as a watering trough and plunged his face in the cool water. When he came up, sputtering and shaking the drops from his hair, he glanced toward the hitching rail at the front of the house. There was a horse standing there.

Jeff rubbed the water out of his eyes and stared again. It was a smallish horse, piebald and dusty. It stood wearily, with head hanging and one hip drooped. From the sheath alongside the old, worn saddle the stock of a rifle protruded.

"By thunder!" Jeff muttered. "It could be my pa!"

He raced for the door, heedless of the field dirt on his cowhide boots.

The man who stood inside, facing Uncle Wash, was built like Jeff himself, tall and lean and straight. His dark hair hung nearly to his shoulders. He wore a frayed, smoke-blackened buckskin hunting shirt, and his long legs, too, were clad in buckskin. On his feet were moccasins.

The voices ceased as Jeff came in. He didn't know what had been said, but from the scowl on his uncle's face he guessed the words hadn't been friendly. The dark man turned with a grin and held out both hands to the boy. Jeff gripped them tight.

"I'm 'most surprised he'd know ye, John," Uncle Wash said peevishly. "I'd ha' took ye fer an Injun, myself. Rigged out like that, ye don't look rightly civilized."

John Barlow laughed, deep and quiet, the way Jeff remembered. "Guess he'd know me, all right," he replied. "We're as like as two peas, except for a couple of inches. You've sure been growing, Jeff. In these two years you must have shot up close to a foot!"

"That's right," Uncle Wash put in. "But growin' don't come cheap. He's nigh et me out o' house an' home."

"Gee, Pa!" said Jeff. "I've been waitin' an' hopin' for you to come back. Did you catch a lot o' fur?"

"I did fair enough," his father answered. "Anyhow I was able to put some money in the bank in St. Louis. Must be nearing suppertime now, and the both of us had best get cleaned up. Where you want me to sleep, Wash?"

"North bedroom," Wash Peters replied sourly, "with Jeff. You an' him kin make out together, I reckon—if you ain't fergot how to sleep in a bed, that is."

John Barlow shouldered his saddlebags, and the two went up the stairs to the little room under the eaves that was Jeff's. While his father scrubbed himself at the wash-basin and put on a clean cotton shirt, the boy sat on the edge of the bed and watched him. It was hard to believe this tanned frontiersman with the whipcord arms was the schoolmaster who had gone west two years before.

Jeff had been under fourteen when his mother died. That was back in Springfield, Illinois, where John Barlow taught. He must have loved his wife very much, for after the funeral he changed. Silent and unsmiling, he went about his work till the school term ended. Then he left Jeff on the farm with Mrs. Barlow's brother Wash, and rode away westward, heading for the unexplored wilderness of the Rockies. All he would say was that he was through with teaching and wanted to be a fur trapper—as far away from towns and people as he could get.

"Wasn't it awful lonesome, Pa?" Jeff asked. "Up there in the high mountains?"

His father smiled. "Oh, not so terrible," he said. "Had a good partner most o' the time. It's a great country out there, son. I want you to see it before it's spoiled."

"Gosh!" Jeff cried. "You mean I can go back with you?"

His father nodded. "That's why I'm here. We'd better go down now."

"But wait, Pa," Jeff begged. "You said 'before it's spoiled.' What's goin' to spoil anything that big?"

John Barlow took his arm firmly and steered him down the stairs. "Don't worry," he said with a grin. "There won't be many changes for a few more years, at least."

Miss Samantha, the sour old maid who kept house for Uncle Wash, was putting supper on the table. She looked sharply at the man and boy, as if expecting signs of dirt around the ears. Disappointed in that, she jerked out a chair, flounced into it, and bowed her head stiffly while Wash Peters mumbled a grace.

They ate in silence for a while. Then the farmer looked up with a frown. "How long do ye aim to hang 'round here, John?" he asked.

"Overnight is all, I reckon. We can be on our way at sunup."

"Ye mean ye're takin' the boy with ye?"

"I am. Do you have a spare horse to sell?"

Wash Peters shook his head. "Don't know's I'd let ye have one if I did," he growled. "Seems to me it's plumb sinful, leadin' a innercent young'un off amongst Injuns an' drunken, godless trappers. How d'ye expect him to amount to anything?"

Jeff's father didn't raise his voice. "I expect him to learn to be a man," he replied quietly. "And I'll have a chance to give him some education, too, now that he's been taken out of school."

"I've had all the trouble an' expense o' raisin' the boy," Uncle Wash complained. "An' now ye want to snatch him away, jest as he's gittin' big enough to be some help."

"I'm grateful to you for taking him in," said the mountain man. "But I don't think there's ever been a day when he hasn't earned his keep and more besides. What you've had, Wash, is a hired hand you didn't have to pay."

The farmer's face flushed red as the wattles of a turkey cock. "You—you trash!" he sputtered. "Say that to me in my own house! I oughta throw ye out this minute!"

Calmly John Barlow ate the last of his pie. "Better take it easy, Wash," he answered. "Getting as mad as that might give you a stroke. Forget I said it. That pony o' mine is tired and hungry, and we're going to have to ride double. So we'll stay the night—in the barn if you prefer—and start for St. Louis in the morning."

Jeff got to his feet. "I'll go take care o' the horse an' give him a bait of oats, Pa," he said. "I don't mind sleeping in the hay."

A few minutes later his father joined him in the barn. He was carrying his saddlebags.

"We don't seem to be too welcome," he told Jeff. "Better go in now, before it's dark, and get your possibles. Put what you own in a sack and bring it out here. Then we won't have to bother 'em again."

The boy obeyed. There weren't many things that belonged to him—just some extra underwear and shirts, a comb, his homespun winter jacket and wool hat, and a faded little tintype of his mother. He packed them in a flour sack, then hesitated a moment and went to the loose board in the corner of the floor. Lifting it, he took out a dozen sheets of paper and a stub of pencil. Some of the paper was covered with sketches he had made—the great pileated woodpecker that had drilled a hole in the buckeye limb outside his window, the new calf born early that spring, Uncle Wash plowing behind his team of mules. Carefully he folded the papers and stowed them in the bag. These things were his own secret. He wasn't sure he wanted to show them even to his father.

It was dusk when he went back to the barn. Uncle Wash was there, milking by lantern light, and Jeff pitched in to help him as usual. Neither of them said a word while the warm white streams of milk drummed in the pails. John Barlow was nowhere in sight. When they finished, Jeff carried the milk to the springhouse and his uncle went back to the kitchen, still silent, his face set in a mulish scowl.

A whippoorwill called insistently from a patch of trees down in the pasture. Jeff heard an answering call close at hand and saw a tall, dark figure there behind the barn. A fragrance of clove pinks came from Miss Samantha's garden as the boy passed it on the way to join his father.

"Kind of a pretty night," John Barlow said. "I'd nearly forgotten what it was like, back here in Illinois. Warm and soft and pleasant. You sure you want to leave it? Even a summer night is different out there. Cold, bright stars overhead, and the wind always blowing and the wolves howling. It's a big, rough, wild country, son."

Jeff needed no time to think it over. "That's where I want to go, Pa," he said, "an' I ain't changed my mind."

His father smiled. "You mean 'haven't,' don't you? We'll have to work on your grammar. It's easy to tell you've missed some schooling.

"But that's not all you'll need to learn," he continued. "I'll have to teach you how to shoot straight and load fast. And there are a million other things you'll find out, mostly from experience. Just staying alive out there in the high plains and in the mountains takes most of a man's time. Meat and firewood and forage for the horses—you can't buy 'em. You have to learn to find 'em. Sometimes it's fifty miles between streams or water holes. Sometimes you get caught in a blizzard and starve and freeze for days. And all the time you have to keep an eye peeled for varmints and Indians. One thing, though—if you come through a year or two o' that and don't lose your scalp, you can call yourself a man."

The boy laughed. "Maybe you're tryin' to skeer me off, Pa," he answered. "But it won't work. I still want to go with you."

His father looked at him soberly. "All right," he said. "So be it. Reckon we'd better bed down and get some sleep."

They went into the barn together and lay down on a pile of old hay in a corner. It was dusty, and Jeff sneezed once before he got comfortable. Small, peaceful noises came to him—the slow sighing of a cow, the creak and thump as one of the mules settled down to rest. Overhead, in the empty hayloft, a mouse squeaked and scurried. Happy in the thought of tomorrow, Jeff drifted off to sleep.

* * * *

His father was already up when he woke at the first gray of coming daylight. The pinto horse, tethered by a long rope, was munching greedily at the fresh grass outside the open barn door.

"Time to move," said John Barlow. "Riding double, we'll have to take it slow, so I want to get a good start before the heat o' the day. We'll find some breakfast along the road."

That was fine as far as Jeff was concerned. He had no particular desire to say good-by to Uncle Wash or Miss Samantha. He washed at the horse trough, drank deep from the spout of the wooden pump, and climbed on the horse behind his father. In a moment they were ambling westward along the rutted dirt road.

Jeff had never been to St. Louis, sixty miles away. He remembered Springfield, of course, but that was the only town of any size he had ever seen. As the sun rose, his heart warmed to a sense of high adventure.

The signs of the beginning day were all around them as they rode. Cattle were being put out to pasture. Hens cackled in the farmyards. Occasionally a dog ran out to bark at the passing strangers.

Two hours and six or eight miles from the Peters' place, they came to a little village where there was a gristmill and a general store. They left the horse at the hitching rail and went into the store.

"Need a few vittles," said Jeff's father to the merchant. "A little corn meal and some crackers and cheese'll do. Maybe a pound o' dried apples if you have 'em."

The man weighed out their purchases. "How 'bout a jug o' whisky fer the road?" he suggested, eying the buckskin-clad trapper. "Prime red-eye, better'n ye'll git out yonder."

"No, thanks," said Barlow. "I don't use it myself, and I doubt if the boy does, either."

"Hmm," replied the storekeeper, still curious. "Stranger in these parts, hain't ye? Goin' fur?"

"St. Louis," said Jeff's father. He laid some money on the counter, took his change and the groceries, and they went out again.

The road forded a stream a mile or two beyond the village. There they turned off into the shade of some trees and ate a cold breakfast while the pinto grazed.

"Don't eat but a few o' those dried apples," John Barlow warned. "Soon as you drink water they'll swell up in your stomach."

With their morning hunger satisfied, they rode on. By noon they had covered close to twenty miles, and the horse was lathered with sweat.

"We'll rest awhile," said the mountain man. "Let the pony cool off before we go on. Ever handled a gun?"

Jeff shook his head. "I wanted to take the shotgun," he said, "an' knock off some crows, but Uncle Wash wouldn't let me."

"Here," said his father, handing him the rifle. "Hold her

easy, and let's see you drill that stump over yonder. She's loaded and the cap's on. Just pull back the hammer with your thumb. Then take aim and squeeze the trigger—not too hard."

Jeff lined up the sights on the stump. At the pressure of his finger there was a satisfying bang and the stock bucked against his shoulder.

"Little high," his father remarked, "but not bad for a first try. You weren't holding quite solid and she jumped a mite. Now I'll show you how to load."

Deftly he poured a small quantity of powder from the horn into the muzzle of the long gun, shook it down, and took a bullet from his pouch. He laid the bullet on a tiny circle of greased linen that came from the patch box in the side of the stock, pressed it into the muzzle with his thumb, and drove it home with a single smooth stroke of the hickory ramrod.

"There," he said. "Soon as I put on the percussion cap, she's ready to shoot again. I've seen hunters do the whole job in a dozen seconds, riding full speed after a buffalo."

"Gosh!" exclaimed Jeff, openmouthed. "Can you do it, too? On horseback, I mean?"

"Not quite that quick, but near enough. There's no time to fool around when you've got a wounded grizzly or a Blackfoot brave coming at you. Here, take another crack at that stump. This time see if you can hit the knot there on the right."

Jeff aimed again, held the rifle firmly, and nicked the left side of the knot.

"Good," said his father. "You'll do after a little more practice. Now swab out the barrel and see if you can load her."

chapter 2

They came in sight of the river toward evening of the second day. From the bluffs they could look across the mile-wide yellow current and see the spires of the city, tiny on the other side. The Mississippi! Jeff drew a deep breath and stared, wide-eyed.

"That's St. Louis, over across," said his father. "We might as well camp here and take the ferry over in the morning."

Sleeping on the ground was no hardship in weather like this. A breeze blew from the west and carried away the mosquitoes. The travelers had eaten heartily in a tavern at noon, and now John Barlow made coffee over a small fire with water from his canteen. They drank it, washing down the last of the crackers and cheese. The mountain man lighted his pipe. It was good to lie there and look at the far-off twinkle of lights in the city.

"Have to get you outfitted, soon as we find a place to stay," said Jeff's father. "Then we'll take a steamboat up the Missouri. There's a new post they call Independence, this side o' the Big Bend. We can pick up some horses there and hit the trail overland to the Platte."

The names fell like music on Jeff's ears. He was full of

questions about the trip, but John Barlow only grinned, puffed at his pipe, and told the boy he'd see soon enough. Before it had been dark an hour they were both asleep.

The sun was up when Jeff woke.

"Roll out, son. Time to shine," his father urged. "We'll wait for breakfast till we get to St. Louis."

The road was steep, going down the bluff, and they went afoot, leading the horse. At the riverbank a steam ferry was being loaded. They went aboard, and soon the moorings were cast off, the whistle tooted, and the little side-wheeler went churning out into the current, its walking beam clanking up and down to the thrust of the engine.

Jeff stood on the forward deck watching the vessel's progress. She had to head far upstream to make up for the steady push of the river. When she was some distance above the city, the pilot swung her bow to the left and she drove across the current crabwise, finally fetching up at the landing on the Missouri side.

A dozen river steamers were tied up along the water front, and among them were smaller craft—skiffs, keelboats, and pirogues. Jeff had never seen or imagined so many people all in one place. Negro stevedores, stripped to the waist, rolled bales and barrels up from the boats to horse-drawn drays. Handsomely dressed passengers waited to board steamers bound for New Orleans or Cincinnati. And picturesque, red-sashed men from the fur brigades gabbed away in what Jeff supposed was French. There were even a few sorry-looking Indians in the throng.

Mounted once more on the pinto, the father and son rode up a broad, dusty street into the town. As one looked at the street signs and the names over the stores, it was easy to remember that St. Louis had once been a French city. There were the Rue Royale and the Rue de l'Eglise, the Rue des Granges and a dilapidated section known as the Vide Poche—the empty pocket.

It was close to the Vide Poche quarter that John Barlow pulled up before a small two-story hotel. A faded sign above the door announced its name as the Laramie House.

"This is where I've stayed before," Jeff's father said. "It's plain but clean. Run by a fellow named McCann. He used to be a trapper till he lost an arm in a fight with the Sioux."

They dismounted and carried their gear into the big room that served as both parlor and bar. The grizzled man behind the counter had an empty sleeve. He looked up and grinned.

"I see you done it," he said in greeting. "Brung the youngster with ye. I got a room saved. Number three, same one ye was in last time. Had any breakfast?"

"Not yet," Barlow answered. "Soon as we've stowed our possibles we'll be down—and hungry!"

They were at a corner table, doing justice to steaming plates of ham and eggs, when a tall, gaunt scarecrow of a man entered and ambled up to the bar. He wore buckskins that were even more weather-stained than John Barlow's and his lank hair was nearly white.

Jeff saw McCann pour the man a drink, then jerk his head toward the table where they sat. The newcomer turned, took a good look, and let out a whoop.

"Wagh!" he cried. "If it ain't Jawn, hisself! Wal, hoss, this shore does shine—an' ye got the boy, too!"

Barlow sprang up and held out his hand, grinning a welcome. "Good to see you, old-timer," he said. "Jeff, this is my partner, Wind River Slim. He taught me most o' what I know. Now I hope he'll take you in hand."

Jeff, on his feet, felt his hand gripped by a paw like iron.

"Nothin' I'd ruther do," said Slim with a chuckle. "Not if he's as smart at l'arnin' as his pappy. Go on an' eat, now. This child'll jest finish his dram."

He squatted on his heels beside their table and sipped noisily at the liquor. Every once in a while he gave his thigh a happy slap and exclaimed, "Wagh!"

"I suppose," said John Barlow, "you've spent all your beaver?"

"Close," Slim cackled. "But not quite all. We better git started soon, though. She's meltin' like snow in a chinook wind."

"We'll be ready quick enough," Barlow replied. "Aim to start outfitting today. I take it you want to come with us?"

Slim rose with alacrity. "Shore do," he said. "Outfittin's fun an' thar's nothin' this coon likes better'n spendin' another man's money! By the way, Jawn, I run into Pete LeBlanc while you was away. Reckon he'd throw in with us if'n we want him."

Barlow looked thoughtful. "For a Frenchy," he commented, "Pete's a pretty good hunter. How floats your stick?"

The question puzzled Jeff for a moment till he figured out it was mountain talk for "How do you feel about it?"

"Sets fine with this child," Slim replied. "Four ain't too many, if we should run into trouble. An' I reckon we'll find enough beaver fer all."

"Good enough," said Jeff's father, rising from the table. "Next time you see him, tell him he's in."

The three of them strolled down the street to the famous gun shop where Jake Hawken made rifles. The proprietor looked up from polishing a curly-maple gun stock and nodded a greeting.

"Jake," said Slim, "here's a young buck needs a Hawken rifle. What ye got on hand?"

The gunsmith shook his head. "Cleaned out right now," he replied. "Some o' Bill Sublette's men was in here an' took the last one. Won't be a new lot ready fer a month."

Jeff was disappointed. "Doesn't anybody else sell guns?" he asked his father.

"Not like these," said Barlow. "Best buffalo guns in the West."

He turned and wandered around the shop, looking at some of the old guns and parts that hung on the walls. He took a long, slim-barreled rifle from its pegs and brushed away the cobwebs.

"What's this one?" he asked.

Hawken glanced at it. "That? Oh, it's an old Kentucky piece a feller brung in here once. Used to be a flintlock an' he wanted her changed to percussion. By the time I got the job done, he was dead. Got knifed in a tavern fight. But I guess you wouldn't want that 'un. She's pretty light. Shoots ball that run forty-five to the pound."

"I dunno," Slim put in. " 'Tain't so much the weight

o' the ball as whar she puts it. Some o' them old Kaintuck rifles was sweet to shoot. This coon thinks he'd like to try her out."

Jake Hawken shrugged. "There's a target in the yard back yonder. Set up fer fifty paces. But I reckon if she holds true at fifty, she's good up to a couple o' hundred. I never fired her myself. See if these bullets fit."

Slim, followed by Jeff and his father, took the ancient rifle outside. The grizzled mountain man swabbed the grease out of the barrel carefully, put in the powder charge and a patched ball, and fitted a percussion cap. He stood back from the target as far as space would allow and lifted the gun, firing at once. As if by magic, a small, dark hole appeared a bare half inch from the bull's-eye.

"She'll do," said Slim. "You try her, Jawn."

Barlow reloaded and took aim. His shot was right in the edge of the little red circle. Finally it was Jeff's turn. He liked the feel of the rifle, light and nicely balanced. With the sights lined up on the bull's-eye, he squeezed the trigger and was amazed at its easy, quick response. With the crack of the report he saw another hole come into view, just above the mark but as close as Slim's. He was proud of his shot, but there were no words of praise.

His father and Slim simply nodded at each other. "Holds true, don't she?" Slim remarked. "Let's find out what he'll take fer her."

Back inside the shop, Slim laid the old rifle back on its pegs. Hawken watched him quizzically. "No good, huh?" he asked.

"Oh, she shoots true enough, for an old relic like that," said John Barlow. "Might do for small game. What would your price be?"

The gunsmith scratched his chin. "Say five plew?" he suggested.

Slim gave a snort. "Ye ought to be glad to get shet of her!" he said. "Fer no more'n it cost ye to change the lock, anyhow. 'Pears like three plew would cover that."

The haggling went on till they finally split the difference. Then Jeff saw his father count out twenty-four dollars and take the gun.

Hawken grinned. "Here," he said. "I've got the bullet mold for her, an' a good powder horn. They're on the prairie."

Jeff didn't know what that meant, but he saw his father take the mold and the horn and shake the gunsmith's hand. "On the prairie," the boy decided, must mean a free gift —something like "on the house."

All the way back to the hotel Slim appeared pleased with his bargaining powers. "Ye picked up a real nice gun," he told Jeff, "at less'n half the goin' price. Jake gits at least ten plew fer one he makes himself."

"What's a plew?" the boy asked, bewildered.

"Used to mean a prime beaver skin," his father explained. "That's back when prices were higher and one top skin was worth six dollars. Comes from a French word—*plus*—meaning an extra good pelt. Nowadays it generally takes four or five skins to make a plew. But figuring in money, a plew is still the same as six dollars."

"An' this coon," said Slim with a sigh, "has seed the day when one lone trapper'd come out o' the mountains with a thousan' plew! Beaver ain't that plenty no more."

John Barlow laughed. "You'll discourage the boy," he said. "We'll find beaver, and we'll trap 'em. All that's wrong with you is that some folks get lazy in their old age. They forget how hard they used to work to bring out a thousand plew."

That afternoon the business of outfitting continued. Jeff wanted buckskins, but the two older men advised against it. They bought a pair of stout moccasins for him and some tough stroud breeches.

"Time enough for buckskins when your cloth things wear out," his father told him. "Making 'em yourself'll give you something to work on when we're snowed in for the winter."

The words made Jeff pause and think. He hadn't quite realized until then that all his time in the Rockies wouldn't be spent in hunting and trapping. "Snowed in for the winter" had a harsh, cold sound, but his father seemed to take it as a matter of course.

Added to the boy's possessions were a good hunting knife and an awl. "An awl looks like a small thing," his father told him, "but you can do a heap o' things with it. Sewing leather, for instance, or making moccasins. Indians think a lot of an awl. It's one o' the first things they ask for in trade."

The final stop was at a blacksmith shop where beaver traps were made. The stock was low at this season of the year. The smith and his helpers forged most of their traps during the winter and sold them to the returning trappers and fur companies when summer came. Only ten good traps were to be had, and John Barlow paid a high price to get them. These were for Jeff. His father and Slim had hidden their traps before they left the mountains—"cached" them, as Slim put it.

The Frenchman, Pete LeBlanc, came to see them at the Laramie House that night. He was a jolly-faced young man, square-built and strong-looking. His broken English amused Jeff, but the boy couldn't help liking him.

"Dese hoss t'ink, by gar, she's tam to start," he announced jovially. "We wanna git to *Roche Jaune* in tam for fall hunt—no?"

"Ain't goin' to the Yellowstone—what you call the *Roche Jaune*—this trip," Slim replied. "Jes' take it easy an' don't git in a sweat. We'll be in beaver country afore the fur's prime."

Jeff left the three men talking and went to bed. He wanted to rise early and see more of the big town.

By six o'clock he was up and dressed, too eager for sightseeing to wait for breakfast. He passed a big Catholic church and went on along a street of stores and business offices. There was a bookshop in the middle of the block—a modest little building with one dusty, small-paned show window. He was almost past it when he glimpsed a painting, set back behind the piles of books. In crude, bright colors it showed the face of an Indian chief, wearing full war paint and a great eagle-feather headdress. Even through the dirty glass he could see that this was no chromo but an original painting on canvas.

At that moment the little old man who owned the shop came up the street with a key in his hand and unlocked the door.

"Interested in good books, young man?" he asked, eying the boy's country attire.

"Not so much books," Jeff answered hesitantly. "It was that picture o' the Injun that took my eye."

"Funny thing," said the old man. "That's been there quite a spell an' not many have even noticed it. Artist fellow named Seymour left it here to pay for some books he wanted. He said it was a portrait of a Pawnee chief."

"I haven't got any money," Jeff told him. "But I'd sure like to take a closer look. Sometimes I draw pictures, an' I wanted to see how he lays his paint on."

The bookseller offered no objection, and for the next half hour the boy stood absorbed, studying every detail of the face—the shadows under the high cheekbones, the somber eyes, the carefully drawn feathers and beadwork.

At last he looked up with a sigh. "Don't suppose it's much use askin' what you'd take for it," he said.

"The price I've put on it is fifty dollars," the old man answered. "That's what Seymour said it was worth, and I expect I can get more'n that if I hang on to it a while longer. Never can tell—he might be famous some day."

Jeff nodded wistfully, then went back to the hotel for breakfast. Fifty dollars! You could buy a horse and saddle for that.

chapter 3

There was little more to be done in preparation for the journey. John Barlow went that morning to purchase a selection of trade goods—mostly small things that could be easily carried. At Chouteau's outfitting establishment Jeff watched him buy a dozen cheap knives, several pounds of colored beads, twenty yards of red and blue calico, and a good-sized package of vermilion. The red powder was highly prized by the Indians, Wind River Slim explained. Its principal use was for painting their faces and chests before a battle.

Slim spent most of the afternoon with Jeff, in the back yard of the Laramie House, showing the boy how to throw a knife.

"Thar's times," he said, "when yer gun ain't loaded an' ye've got to defend yerself right now. I mind me oncet on the Little Missouri I'd laid down my rifle an' was puttin' wood on the fire. Looked up an' seen a sneakin' Dakota brave fixin' to steal the gun. No time to do anythin' but let fly with the knife. Pinned him right in the arm."

"What happened then?" Jeff asked.

"Nothin' much. He let out a yell an' high-tailed it fer the brush. Never come 'round to bother me again."

Jeff's coordination was good and he learned quickly. By suppertime he could flick his arm over in a split second and drive the point of the blade into a wooden post twenty feet away.

A steamboat for the Missouri River would leave at ten next morning, they learned. Before going to bed, Jeff and his father packed their "possibles," and soon after breakfast they were on their way to the water front, loaded down with their rifles and bags. The pinto horse, on a lead rope, carried the traps and still more equipment. He wouldn't be going with them, for they planned to purchase their mounts and pack animals at Independence. A stableboy from the inn went with them to take the pony back.

They loaded everything on the foredeck of the steamboat, where the space was already crowded with the belongings of twenty or thirty other travelers. There were staterooms on the upper deck, but these were reserved for more elegant passengers—gentlemen in tall beaver hats and pretty ladies in wide-skirted crinolines. Jeff stared up at them as they came aboard, marveling at the men's courtly manners and the tinkling, affected laughter of the ladies.

There was still a third class of passengers. These were men without money, working their way upriver by loading wood for the steam boiler. The boat made a stop every few hours at landings where the fuel had been piled up, and the roustabouts carried it aboard, cursed by the officers for being slow or clumsy.

Other delays were caused by snags, "sawyers," and shifting, treacherous sand bars. A sawyer, Jeff discovered, was a tree trunk with the branches still on, hidden beneath the muddy yellow surface. Disturbed in the place where it had lodged, it might turn over suddenly, thrusting a jagged limb through the boat's shallow bottom. Luckily they didn't run onto one, but sand bars were another matter.

Over and over again, during the three-day voyage, the vessel ran hard aground in what looked as if it should be the main channel. This wasn't disastrous—just time-consuming. After an hour or less the loose sand would scour away from under the keel and the boat could be backed off.

The men on the foredeck ate whatever they had brought with them, heating stew or coffee in pots set against the side of the firebox, amidships. By the time they reached their destination, Jeff was thoroughly tired of steamboat travel.

It was midmorning of a hot June day when they came within sight of Independence. The new post lay on the south bank of the broad, muddy river. It had a raw, unfinished look. Three or four buildings had been thrown together out of logs and rough boards. There was a long, low structure that served as a trading center, two saloons, and a blacksmith shop. There were also two corrals.

Behind the post, on higher ground, were a score of Indian lodges—not the cone-shaped tepees Jeff had seen in pictures, but low, rounded huts of bark, poles, and sod.

"Kaws," said John Barlow briefly. "Won't fight unless they're drunk, but keep an eye on your gear. They'll steal you blind, give 'em half a chance."

They carried their belongings ashore and put everything in a compact pile.

"Let's git some hosses an' move out today," Slim urged. "We could git fur enough from here to camp out o' range o' Injuns."

Barlow nodded. "Suits me," he said. "Pete—will you stand guard over this stuff while we do the trading? I reckon you want three horses, same as the rest of us."

LeBlanc was perfectly willing to leave the buying to the others. "Me—I wan' beeg, strong hoss for ride," he said with a grin. "I'm heavy man!"

He handed over some money from a sack tucked inside his shirt, and Barlow and Slim, with Jeff trailing after them, walked to the nearest corral. The horse-trader was a fat, red-faced man in city clothes.

"Hiya, gents," he greeted them. "Lookin' fer hosses? I've got the best—all sound, well-broke stock. Take ye clear to Oregon if so be ye're headed that-a-way."

The two mountain men eyed him coldly, looked over the horses without comment, then strolled on to see what was in the second corral. There they found a lean, weather-beaten plainsman in charge. He looked at Slim and his eyes lighted up.

"Wal," he cried, "you ol' coyote! Hain't had a sight o' ye since the year o' the first rendezvous on the Seeds-kee-dee! Still trappin'?"

Slim grabbed him by the arms. "Wagh!" he said. "Joe Blatcher! Sellin' crowbait to onsuspectin' trappers, huh? Thought you was a shore-'nough mountain man."

He introduced his companions and the trading started. In spite of some slighting remarks by Slim, the horses in Blatcher's corral were far better than the first lot, even to Jeff's unpracticed eye. Most of them were Indian ponies, tough and wiry but in good flesh. There were a few mules and two or three bigger-boned animals that might have been farm horses. It was one of these that Barlow bought for Pete LeBlanc.

Jeff had been looking wishfully at a slim-legged, quick-moving buckskin, and was happy when his father asked its price.

"Now that there," said Blatcher proudly, "is a genu-wine buffler hoss. Got him off a Pawnee chief. Cost me a hull gallon o' trade liquor an' three blankets, but I reckon I'd sell him fer 'round six plew."

After some dickering, Barlow got the pony for thirty dollars. Most of the others were cheaper, but there were saddles also to be bought. In the end they wound up with a mount and two pack horses for each of them, including Pete, and settled for a total of something over four hundred dollars. To Jeff's delight the buckskin was allotted to him.

He made friends with the pony, cinched the saddle, took the single rein of the hackamore in his hand, and started to scramble aboard.

"Hold on!" His father checked him. "You're getting on from the left, like a town boy. You'll never see an Indian or a real mountain man do that—we always take the right-hand side."

"What difference does it make?" Jeff asked.

"None in particular. Only you try to mount an Indian pony from the left and he's liable to buck you into the middle o' next week. He's just not used to it. Get on now and see how he does."

Jeff put his right foot in the stirrup, swung his left over the cantle, and settled in his seat. At a touch of his moccasin heel the buckskin set off at an easy lope. Jeff had been told to guide the pony by the pressure of his knees, rather than trying to do it with the rein. He experimented and found his mount responded instantly.

"Come on, boy," his father called with a laugh. "Quit sashaying around and let's get something to eat. We want to reach a good camping place before dark."

There was no fuel handy except four-foot logs that belonged to the steamboat company, so Jeff went off to see what he could find in the way of firewood. He had to walk some distance, and before he returned with an armful of dry sticks, he was surrounded by begging Indians and squaws. Shaking his head and striding toward the post, he managed to keep them off. His mental picture of strong, fearless redmen was badly shattered by these first specimens. They gave off a heavy odor of dirt and rancid grease that fairly turned his stomach.

With Pete's help he built a small fire and the meal was soon cooked. When they had eaten, they roped their gear on the back of the extra ponies and set off in single file.

John Barlow led the way. Slim, after a quick visit to one of the saloons with his friend Blatcher, brought up the rear. Each man had the lead ropes of two pack horses tied to his saddle pommel, and each carried his rifle in a leather scabbard attached to the saddle in front of his knee. Other necessities, such as powder horns, bullet pouches, and sheath knives, were slung on thongs over their shoulders or fastened to the belts they wore outside their hunting shirts. Slim and Pete also had heavy buffalo pistols tucked in their waistbands.

The trail led west by south, away from the river. Soon they came to wooded country where big hardwood trees gave some shade from the afternoon sun. After they had been riding two or three hours, John Barlow reined in his black pony and handed over the lead ropes to Jeff.

"Go ahead," he said. "The trail's easy to follow here. I aim to ride off a bit and try to get us some meat."

A moment later Slim followed his example, taking the opposite flank, and Jeff and Pete were left to herd the eight pack animals along. The Frenchman caught a glimpse of Jeff's disconsolate face and chuckled.

"Don' worry, boy," he said. "Dere's long way to go. You an' me—we get chance for hunt some tam pretty queek."

A faraway rifle shot sounded from off at the left where Jeff's father had gone. Two or three minutes later another came from the right.

"We get good supper tonight, by gar!" said Pete. "Fresh meat for sure!"

Shortly they left the woods and found themselves in rolling meadow country where the grass stood high. The horses slowed to grab at mouthfuls of it as they went along. After half an hour Jeff saw his father riding toward them over a rise. Something bulky lay across his horse's withers, and as he cantered nearer, the boy could make out the carcass of a deer.

"She's good place for hunt," Pete commented. "All tam now we have plenty meat."

A few minutes later Slim also rejoined the cavalcade. He held up a fat turkey gobbler by the legs and had opened his mouth to do a little bragging when he caught sight of the deer.

"Wal, anyways," he remarked, "we kin eat turkey fer dessert."

They pushed on another five or six miles before sunset. At a small stream, where cottonwoods grew along the banks, they halted for the night. Pete unloaded and picketed the horses, Jeff gathered firewood, and the two hunters cleaned their game. The fresh meat, broiled on green sticks over the blaze, tasted wonderful to the boy. No bread or vegetables went with it, but Slim assured him that meat alone was a complete diet.

"Ye kin stuff yerself to bustin'," he said, "an' never git a bellyache. 'Course, in the spring a few greens go good. But I've lived on nothin' but buffler fer two months runnin' an' felt powerful 'nuff to lick a hull passel o' wildcats single-handed."

After supper they spread their blankets around the dying fire and Jeff lay on his back, looking up at the stars. Out here on the plains, away from farms and settlements, they seemed brighter and more numerous.

Wind River Slim told a couple of tall tales about his Indian-fighting days and Pete played some old French tunes on a little tin flute. Then John Barlow rose and stretched.

"I suppose we'd better keep a watch," he said, "with Kaws around. All I'm worried about is the horses. Jeff, you take the first turn. Wake me up in a couple of hours. Keep your rifle ready but don't use it unless you're dead sure there's trouble."

The responsibility weighed on Jeff at first. He could hear the gentle snoring of his companions and, now and then, a crackle from the dying fire. The wind made a steady rustling in the leaves of the cottonwoods. Time seemed to drag slowly. He had no watch, but he took a sight on a group of stars to the east and decided that when they had wheeled nearly overhead, it would be time to rouse his father.

For an hour he sat still, the rifle cradled across his knees, and thought of the hard farm life he had left behind. Trapping wouldn't be easy either, but he would be free—his own man. Suddenly he heard a horse snort close by, and from somewhere out on the prairie came the howl of a coyote. The quavering call was echoed from nearer at hand, and Jeff got to his feet, all his senses alert.

If it was just coyotes, he knew there was nothing to worry about. But Slim had told him Indians sometimes signaled each other that way. He crouched low and went silently toward the picketed ponies. The fire had died to ashes now, and his eyes were accustomed to the faint light of the stars. Was that something moving, just to the left of the horse herd?

Without a sound he waited. Then he was sure the dark figure moved, creeping closer to the animals. There was a small click as he cocked the rifle, and the shape stopped moving, sinking lower in the grass.

"Who's there?" Jeff yelled. "Get out or I'll shoot!"

He aimed just above the intruder and pulled the trigger. At the report he saw a man spring up and scuttle away. Then his father came hurrying to join him.

"It was an Injun," said Jeff with a shiver. "He was on his hands an' knees, tryin' to get close to the horses."

"Did you hit him?" John Barlow asked.

"No, I aimed over his head. He sure made tracks, though, when I shot."

They listened for a moment and heard the distant pounding of hoofs. "Two of 'em, sounds like," the older man commented. "I don't think we'll be bothered any more tonight. You did just right, son. Now go get some sleep. I'll take over."

No doubt the advice about sleep was sensible, but Jeff lay on his blanket a long time before his eyes would close. He was glad he hadn't aimed lower. It would have been a heavy load on his conscience to have killed a man—even a Kaw bent on stealing horses. The warning shot had served its purpose. The prowlers weren't likely to return, knowing the camp was well guarded. At last, with a yawn, the boy rolled over and was almost instantly asleep.

chapter 4

Wind River Slim teased Jeff a little about the affair next morning. "Too bad ye ain't a better shot, hoss," he told him with a shake of the head. "Been a good way to start out, with Injun ha'r a-danglin' from yer belt."

"Leave the boy alone," Barlow ordered sternly. "He used good sense. A man doesn't have to take scalps to prove he's fit for the trail."

"Jest havin' my fun, Jawn," the old mountain man replied. " 'Twon't hurt him to have some o' the swellin' took down. Reckon I'd ha' done the same as him if'n I'd been thar."

They had more venison for breakfast, gulped down some tea, and saddled their horses. Beyond the stream the country began changing little by little. There were fewer trees and the rolling prairie lay ahead, mile on mile, as far as the eye could see. Toward noon they sighted a small band of antelope off on a rise, half a mile away.

"Lemme go get one, Pa," Jeff begged. "I haven't had a chance to shoot anything yet."

"Ye'd never git close, ridin' out thar," Slim put in. " 'Sides, a pronghorn's sech a skinny leetle thing it's hardly wuth the powder an' ball. This coon'd jest as soon eat jack rabbit."

John Barlow pulled up and handed the lead ropes to Slim. "I'll take Jeff out an' show him how to make 'em come," he said. "Some day he might have to know the trick or go hungry."

The father and son dismounted, took their rifles, and walked a hundred yards or so in the direction of the antelope. There John Barlow lay down in the grass and motioned to Jeff to do the same. From his hunting shirt he took a scrap of bright red cloth a foot square. Tying it to the muzzle of his Hawken, he started waving it slowly over his head.

"Keep your eye on 'em," he told Jeff. "See what happens."

Through the grass stalks the boy could see two or three of the graceful creatures standing like statues, heads up, looking their way. Then they began coming nearer, a few yards at a time, leaping high above the grass for a better view.

"Got a heap o' curiosity," Jeff's father whispered. "They'll come every time to see something they don't understand."

At last one of the animals was within what Jeff thought was easy range. It was a young buck with spike horns. He could see the dark stripe across the white of the throat and the lifted nose that twitched as it tried to catch their scent. The boy lay on his stomach, his left elbow on the ground as a rest for the rifle.

"Go ahead," he heard his father breathe. "Aim for the chest."

He squeezed the trigger and saw the pronghorn leap straight up. As it fell, the others turned their white rumps and sped off so fast his eye could hardly follow.

"Nice shot," said John Barlow. "Looks like a clean hit to the heart."

When they reached it, the antelope was dead, a crumpled thing there in the grass, looking small and pitiful. Jeff's pride was mixed with a measure of regret as he watched his father slit the throat to bleed it.

"They're pretty things," said Barlow. "After this I hope you'll never want to shoot one unless you really need the meat."

He slung the light carcass over his shoulder, and they walked back to rejoin the others.

Pete grinned and nodded, and Slim eyed the heart shot with approval. "Take it all back," he told Jeff. "Reckon you'd ha' drilled that Injun the same way, if'n you'd been a mind to."

They swung northwest again that afternoon and camped for the evening in a cottonwood grove on the bank of the Kaw River. Once more they stood watches, but no Indians came to disturb them. In the morning they urged the horses into the broad, shallow ford and went over without mishap. Jeff wondered if all the rivers they had to cross would be as easy as that.

He found out a day later at the Vermilion. There had been a heavy thunderstorm that started just before sunset and deluged their camping place with several inches of rain. Fortunately, the air stayed warm, for they were drenched to the skin and such sleeping as they managed to do was in sopping wet blankets. It took two hours of hot sun the next morning to dry them out enough to travel.

Ordinarily the Vermilion wasn't much of a river. When they reached it, however, they found it running high and fast and nearly as wide as the Kaw.

"Hold the hosses here," Slim advised, "an' let me try her out. This is whar the ford ought to be."

He rode his rangy roan into the yellow flood and was halfway across before the horse lost its footing. For the next minute they could see him hanging onto the pony's mane and holding his rifle over his head as he yelled encouragement to the swimming animal. Then he was out of the deep current and climbing to reach the farther bank. There he dismounted and waved his arm to them in a beckoning gesture.

"All right," said John Barlow, "here we go. Stay close to me, Jeff, an' hang on tight. That buckskin'll get you through."

The boy took the rifle from its sheath and held it high, as he saw the others do. His pony seemed to have no fear of the hurrying water. It snorted once, then plunged in, dragging the led horses behind. Jeff pulled up his knees and crouched tensely in the saddle. They reached midstream. Then he felt the buckskin settle deeper in the water and begin to swim. The pack horses, with less weight on their backs, forged up abreast, their nostrils flaring and eyes rolling in terror. At last they reached shallower water. The buckskin found a footing and scrambled forward eagerly.

When LeBlanc's big bay came puffing up the bank, they all dismounted, unsaddled, and let the horses shake themselves and roll.

"How's your powder?" Jeff's father asked. "Keep it dry, did you?"

The boy had forgotten about it, but the horn was slung on a thong over his shoulder and he didn't think the water had come much above his waist. He checked it and found the stopper tight.

"You're lucky," said Barlow. "Next time hold it overhead with your gun."

It was another long day's ride to the Big Blue. By the time they reached it, the effects of the cloudburst had passed, and they made the crossing without trouble. The ford was above the fork where the Little Blue came in, and for the next week they plodded up the valley of that river. Sometimes the trail ran within sight of the cottonwood-fringed banks. More often it cut through empty, rolling country where there was little water and no game but prairie chickens and jack rabbits.

Most of the time, now, Slim or Barlow rode well in advance, leaving the others to bring the horses. They had reached the fringe of Indian country, occasionally crossed by roving bands of Pawnees, and daily scouting was a necessary precaution.

When they passed the headwaters of the Little Blue, the land grew dry and dusty. Grass for the horses was hard to find, and there was no fuel except little patches of greasewood that burned out after a quick flare. Luckily Slim recalled that a small water hole lay a few miles south, and they camped there.

"Fill your canteen," Jeff's father counseled. "It'll be a long, dry haul across to the Platte."

The mud around the water hole was dotted with the tracks of coyote and antelope, and the water itself was stagnant, with a greenish scum. Jeff made a face after he tasted it, but the horses drank with no ill effects, so he guessed it wouldn't hurt him.

The only meat they had that night was a pair of prairie chickens Slim had shot.

"Doggone it," Jeff grumbled after supper, "how soon do we get to buffalo country?"

"No way o' tellin'," the old mountain man answered. "An' if I knowed whar the buffler was any time I wanted 'em, I could be the grand chief of all the Injuns in creation. Thar's somethin' spooky about a herd o' buffler. They move accordin' to no plan ever figgered out by a human. Even the medicine men git fooled, an' that's s'posed to be their main business—guidin' the tribe to buffler."

Next day they rode on doggedly, hour after hour, and in midafternoon Jeff saw what looked like a lofty ridge looming ahead.

"Hey, Pa," he called. "Is that the Rocky Mountains?"

His father chuckled. "Don't see any snow on the tops, do you? No, son, those are just sand hills—what they call the coast o' the Platte."

Another hour and they had come to the summit of the dunes—wind-drifted piles of sand, held together by straggling grass and cactus. Spread out before them was the vastest, most desolate country Jeff had ever seen. Beyond the broad river it lay, endless and forbidding, league on league of it, to the edge of the world. It made him feel small and helpless.

"Gosh, Pa," he said. "She's awful big, ain't—isn't she?"

There were a few sparse cottonwoods in the bottoms along the river and more on the low islands in midstream. They were able to make a real fire that night. Over it they cooked a stew of jack-rabbit meat, provided by Slim.

" 'Tain't a banquet," he admitted, "but better'n a plumb empty stomach. What would ye say is the best eatin' there is, Jawn?"

"Hump rib of a nice young buffalo cow would suit me," Jeff's father replied.

"Da's right," Pete LeBlanc put in. "But me—I lak de pork chop bes'—w'at you get in St. Louis."

"Huh!" Slim snorted. "Trust a Frenchie—a lard-eater—to pick hog meat! Now lemme tell ye. The slickest grub this hoss ever et was painter—that's right—mountain lion. Better'n any b'ar or buffler."

Jeff didn't know whether to laugh or not. It sounded like a joke, though he learned later that the veteran mountain man had meant every word of it. Meanwhile, he chewed on the stringy, tasteless meat that was in the pot.

They moved on the next day, keeping to the south bank

of the Platte. Soon the fringing cottonwoods disappeared. There was no shade from the fierce midsummer sun, no wood except a rare driftwood log. Each morning they filled their canteens and watered the horses at the river, then followed the faint trail across endless sand flats, patched with white alkali dust. The only grazing they found was a few clumps of grass, brown now and dry. And the only fuel for their cooking fires was buffalo chips, lying scattered everywhere along the way. The job of gathering them naturally fell to Jeff, as the boy of the party.

That was a hard, miserable week for all of them. The ponies grew gaunt from lack of forage. Even Jeff's buckskin, usually so mettlesome and willing, seemed to be listless and tired. At last, on the twenty-first day out of Independence, they neared the Forks of the Platte.

A big, sandy island had formed in the middle of the river a few miles below where the North and South Platte came together. There was grass there, and a few trees. Also they found evidences that a band of Indians had camped there not very long before.

"Crows," Slim announced, studying the sign. "Been gone five-six days, I reckon. Prob'ly headin' upstream, lookin' fer buffler."

The trappers stayed two days on the island, resting their horses. On the evening of the second day Jeff's father came back from a long scouting trip to the north with a bundle of meat across his saddle. He had found an old, lone buffalo bull, cast off by the herd. And he had brought back the hump meat, the tongue, and the liver—the only parts not too tough to eat.

It was Jeff's first introduction to the staple food of the Plains. After their sketchy diet of the past week he thought it tasted excellent, though the others considered it pretty poor stuff.

"One thing," said Wind River Slim. "That bull ain't

been alone too long or the lobo wolves would ha' had him by now. The rest o' the herd's likely jest a few days' ride from here."

They crossed from the island to the north bank next morning, following the trail left by the Indian hunting party.

"Gen'ally," Slim told Jeff, "ye'll find Crows are friendly Injuns. This is their country, but white men kin 'most always buy hosses from 'em, an' pass through without losin' their ha'r."

More grass grew along the way now, and it was buffalo grass, hardy and succulent, on which the ponies flourished. After two days John Barlow, scouting on ahead, rode back to report he had sighted Indian tepees.

"It's a small band," he said. "Only a few lodges, an' no sign o' women or children around. I guess you were right, Slim—it's a hunting party."

"Wal," the older man replied, "we kin circle on past 'em. Or we kin ride in fer a parley if'n ye're a mind. Mebbe I'd better take a look-see. I'm acquainted with a few o' the Crows an' I reckon we'd be treated fine."

Before sunset he appeared again on the top of a rise and waved them on with his arm. When they rode up, he was looking pleased with himself.

"We're in luck," he said. "White Calf's leadin' 'em, an' he's an old friend o' mine. They've spotted buffler, too. We're invited to stay 'round an' take part in the hunt."

John Barlow agreed they should accept the invitation. "Let's go ahead and make camp near 'em," he said. "I'd like Jeff to get a look at some real Indians."

Two or three miles farther on they came to the Crow encampment. Barlow and Slim dismounted and walked toward the tepees, unarmed, their right hands raised in a sign of peace. Jeff could see a tall, well-built Indian in a feather headdress moving out to meet them. There was talk

for a few minutes, mostly in sign language, and then his father returned and told Pete and Jeff to make camp where they were.

"No need to guard the horses," he added. "Just picket 'em. The Crows have got more than they need. Come on, we're invited to supper. Bring your rifles and possibles, but leave everything else here."

He selected a few gifts from the bundle of trade goods and led the way back to the skin tents, now looming dark against the pink sky in the west.

chapter 5

White Calf met them and motioned the newcomers to sit down in the circle around the fire. A dozen warriors were already seated there with Slim, while two or three youngsters, no older than Jeff, looked after the cooking.

The chief lighted a long pipe with a coal from the fire, lifted the stem toward the sky, pointed it to the ground, then to either side. After a puff or two he passed it to Slim, who sat next to him. The old trapper took his turn and solemnly handed the pipe to John Barlow. When it came to Jeff, he took a small, careful puff and nearly choked on the rank smoke.

"Act as if you liked it," his father warned in a low voice. "This is serious business and we've got to be polite."

Jeff managed to keep his face straight, but he was glad to pass the pipe along to Pete LeBlanc. When it had gone around the full circle, White Calf rose ceremoniously and made a speech. He spoke slowly, accompanying his guttural words with "hand-talk." It was the first time Jeff had seen the sign language of the Plains Indians. His father translated for him under his breath.

"He says the Great Spirit has helped them spot buffalo," he whispered. "They've sent for their squaws and old men to come up and do the skinning. Ought to be here in one more sun. Then the hunt starts. We're invited to hunt with 'em if we want to wait."

"Hey!" Jeff murmured. "Can we?"

Slim looked at Barlow with a question and got a nod in return. After the chief had sat down, he unfolded his lanky body and rose to answer. He spoke haltingly in the Crow tongue, using his hands to make his meaning clear. The message was brief. The Indians' white brothers, Slim told them, would take it as an honor to join them in the killing of the buffalo.

Then John Barlow got up, seconded Slim's remarks, and produced the gifts, which he laid soberly at White Calf's feet. That made everybody happy. More speeches followed, and before it was all over, Jeff was so sleepy he could hardly keep his eyes open. The food had been good—choice parts of cow buffalo—but the amount he had eaten added to his drowsiness.

At last the parley broke up and the white men went back to their blankets. As Barlow had prophesied, their horses and gear were undisturbed.

"Too bad to lose a hull day," Slim remarked at breakfast next morning. "But they wouldn't like it if we pushed on an' shot some buffler—mebbe spooked the herd. Anyhow, it's a chance fer the young'un here to see what an Injun buffler hunt is like."

"We've got time enough," Jeff's father agreed. "The fur won't be prime for another two or three months. Too bad we haven't any bows an' arrows. That's the way to kill buffalo."

"Reckon the boy'll make out," said Slim. "He kin shoot straight enough, even if his gun's a mite light. All is, Jeff, ye want to hold low on a buffler. Thar's a light patch back o' the foreleg whar the ha'r's wore off. 'Bout a hand's breadth above the brisket—that's whar the heart lies."

Jeff cleaned his rifle carefully and made sure he had enough powder, ball, and caps. The others were making their own preparations. Meanwhile, the horses munched at the curly buffalo grass, grateful for the hours of rest.

Shortly before noon, when Jeff's patience was wearing thin, they sighted a cloud of dust coming up from the east. Over the rise appeared a line of twenty or thirty ponies. Most of them were pulling travois—each made of two long poles with the forward ends lashed to the horses' girths and the rear ends trailing on the ground. On these were tied folded tepees, robes, and cooking utensils. Plodding through the dust beside the ponies Jeff saw squaws and children and old men. A few mounted braves rode with them as a guard.

They came down into the bottoms by the river and immediately the tents began to spring up. From long practice the women were quick and clever at this task. Half a dozen lodgepoles formed the framework, leaning together at the top and tied in place with thongs. Then the pale-tanned buffalo hides, sewed together with sinews, were thrown around the poles, pulled flat, and straightened. On the front side of each tepee the edges were laced, leaving a flap at the bottom for an entrance. Some of the lodges, Jeff saw with interest, had crudely painted designs on them—stripes, suns, pictures of horses or buffalo.

While the squaws bustled about their work, the children played and the men rested, sitting aloof from the turmoil. Around and through the camp ran lean, yellow mongrel dogs.

About two o'clock the Crow braves bestirred themselves. Slim watched them for a moment and told his companions it was time to catch the ponies and saddle up. By the time they rode to the Crow camp all the Indian hunters were mounted. The chief's son, a lean young buck named Running Wolf, led the way westward.

Within half an hour they saw the scout who had been keeping the buffalo in view. He waved his arm in a circle northward, indicating that they should cut around the herd and come in from downwind. With the horses at a trot they made a wide circuit, then halted while they were still hidden by a sand hill.

Barlow and Slim dismounted and crawled to the crest with the Indians. When they came back, the report was good.

"Wind's still from the south," said Jeff's father, "and they don't know we're around. It's a small herd—maybe five hundred—and pretty well scattered. Nearest ones are less'n a quarter of a mile away. Watch the Crows, Jeff, and see what they do. Then, when you've picked a young cow, ride alongside and stay with her till you get a good shot."

At a signal from Running Wolf, the whole party mounted and raced over the rise. Pounding along in the midst of them, Jeff saw the Indian hunters string their short, powerful bows and take broad-tipped arrows from their quivers. Ahead, the buffalo had been roused from their grazing and were starting to run at a lumbering gait that was faster than it looked.

His first sight of the big, dark, shaggy beasts had sent a wild excitement coursing through Jeff's veins. He had no need to urge the buckskin. As the trader had said, this was a real buffalo horse, trained to the hunt. By the time they caught up with the stragglers of the herd, Jeff was going neck-and-neck with Running Wolf.

He held his rifle ready. Just ahead of him was a sleek cow, and the pony veered to the animal's left without being guided. When he was a dozen feet away, Jeff pointed the rifle at the white patch behind her shoulder and fired. At that range he could hardly have missed. The cow stumbled, galloped on a stride or two and turned a somersault, landing on her back.

Jeff would have stopped to gloat over his prize, but the buckskin was racing on in pursuit of another cow. Hastily the boy reloaded his rifle, glad now that he had practiced the trick on horseback. Around him he could hear the whoops of warriors and the reports of rifles and pistols. They were fairly into the herd now, but the pony threaded his way through, sure-footed, keeping abreast of the cow he had chosen.

Jeff wished then that he had a bow and arrow. He was crowded so close in the rush of buffalo that he couldn't get a shot at the heart spot behind the foreleg. In desperation he tried what seemed to be the only other course and aimed down at the shoulder to the left of the cow's hump. At the instant he pulled the trigger a big bull jostled against his leg and the bullet flew wild.

Frustrated, Jeff tugged at the hackamore rein, hoping to get free of the crush of buffalo. Cleverly the buckskin pushed sidewise, letting the herd thunder past. Then, to the boy's amazement, he saw another cow down, a short

distance to his right. There was no arrow in her side. And none of the other white men was near him. By sheer luck the second bullet he had fired must have gone over the target and hit the other cow in a vital spot.

The Crow hunters were far away now, still hotly pursuing the stampeding buffalo. On the prairie around him Jeff could count nearly twenty fallen animals, and his father and Pete were standing above two of them. Slim must have gone on with the Indians.

The buckskin pony was still full of run and wanted to continue the chase, but Jeff rode him back to the two men. The throat of one cow had been cut, and Pete LeBlanc was catching the blood in his canteen. The sight shocked Jeff. He hadn't realized buffalo hunting was such a gory business, but he continued to watch as the men went on with their work.

The dead cow had fallen on her stomach. Now they pulled her legs out so that she lay spread-eagled. Starting at the neck, forward of the hump, John Barlow slit the hide down the middle of the back with his big sheath knife. The skin was pulled away to either side, and the hump ribs were cut out, along with some of the loin. When the tongue and the liver had also been taken, the choice meat was rolled in the hide and the rest of the carcass left where it lay.

"Pete and I each got one," Jeff's father told him. "How'd you make out?"

"Two," said Jeff proudly. "Two nice fat cows!"

To his surprise, his father frowned. "You ought to know," he said, "we can't carry all that meat, and it would spoil anyhow in this hot weather. I'm glad you got your chance to shoot one, but it's too bad you killed the second. What we'd better do is make a gift of 'em to the Indians."

Jeff's face fell. "Couldn't I just take the robe from one?" he begged. "It'd be something to keep me warm in the winter."

"Wait till fall, when the hair thickens up," his father replied. "Don't worry—we'll see plenty more buffalo."

The squaws had waited beyond the ridge till the hunt was well under way. Now they came hurrying out, riding or leading a dozen pack ponies. At once they set to work skinning out the dead buffalo. Each brave had his own colored arrow feathers, so it wasn't hard for the women to identify their husbands' kills. They laughed and chattered over the bloody task, gleeful over the amount of meat.

John Barlow asked Jeff to lead him to his two cows. In sign language he told the nearest squaws that these animals were a gift from the young white hunter. They smiled at Jeff, and in the light of their admiring glances he felt better about the affair.

Soon the riders returned, whooping with joy, for it had been a fine hunt. Slim was with them, and he carried a bundle of meat across his horse's rump. He heard about Jeff's exploit without comment. It was only as they started back to camp that he spoke to the boy.

"A real hunter," he said, "never kills more meat'n he knows he kin use. Reckon I'd ha' done the same at yore age, but now ye've l'arned, thar'll be no more excuse fer it. Anyhow, the Injuns'll be glad to git them two extry cows. They'll be eatin' buffler till they nigh bust tonight."

It was after sunset as they rode northward over the rise. Already the ravens and buzzards were at work on the stripped carcasses. The coyotes circled hungrily, and in the distance they could see large gray wolves waiting for the Indian women to depart. By morning there would be little left but bare bones.

As soon as the fire was blazing, Pete and Slim began to prepare supper. Jeff saw them pour the blood from the canteen into the pot. Then they added some chopped liver and the marrow from a big leg bone. Shuddering, he resolved to have none of it. But when it came steaming from the fire and he caught its rich aroma, he was suddenly hungry. It turned out to be as delicious as any food he had ever tasted. A big plate of it was followed by the sweet meat of a hump rib. He tumbled into his blanket so stuffed he could barely stagger.

Even though Jeff was healthily tired and full of food, sleep was a long time coming. Over in the Crow camp the feast went on until after midnight, and it was accompanied by whoops and howls, rhythmic chanting and the throb of drums, as the hunters danced and bragged of their prowess.

The sun was well above the horizon when Jeff woke. He found the others already up and breakfast cooking. Oddly enough, his stomach felt fine in spite of last night's gorging. He ate again with a good appetite, helped pack and saddle up, and was soon ready for the trail.

They rode westward past the Indian encampment.

Drugged by a surfeit of food, not a man, woman, or child was stirring there. Even the dogs, usually so noisy, slept in the shade of the tepees with bloated stomachs.

Slim chuckled. "Good thing we ain't a party o' Sioux or Blackfeet on the warpath," he said. "They'd all ha' lost their ha'r by now."

For several more days they followed the northern bank of the river. The country was beginning to change now, for they were in the high plains, climbing gradually all the way. Nights were chilly in the thin, dry air, and the sky seemed vaster, the stars colder and brighter. One morning as they set out with the sunrise at their backs, Jeff saw a far-off gleam of white ahead. He pointed excitedly and his father nodded.

"That's snow," he said. "The Laramie Range. But it's still a hundred miles ahead. We'll be coming to Chimney Rock pretty soon, and from there on you'll think you're really in the mountains."

Each day Slim or John Barlow scouted off into the hills and brought back game. Sometimes Jeff went with them. There were small, scattered herds of buffalo all around them, and when variety was wanted, it was easy enough to knock over a prairie chicken—a "fool-hen" as Slim called the bird.

The soft rock formation near the river was worn into strange shapes known as buttes. Most of them were like huge table tops with sheer cliffs for sides. One stood slim and tall, and it was easy to see why it bore the name of Chimney Rock. The day after they passed it, Jeff rode to the top of a high bluff and looked out on range after range of snowy peaks—north, west, and south. With a pounding heart he knew he had come at last to the threshold of the Rockies.

chapter 6

As it came down from the high country into the foothills, the North Fork of the Platte was full of falls and tumbling rapids. Once or twice they forded the river to the southern bank, finding the north side blocked by cliffs or fallen rock. But still they continued to climb steadily, day after day.

It was beside a stream called Deer Creek, flowing in from the south, that they stayed over a day to rest the horses. Grass had been sparse, eaten off by the buffalo. But here in the little valley there was shade and grass and good clear water. Jeff went hunting up the creek with Slim that morning. They moved on foot, going quietly through the brush and trees. Jays and magpies chattered at their approach, and the old hunter motioned to Jeff to sit still with him on a log until the birds quieted down.

"Nothin's goin' to come to drink as long as they're squawkin'," he whispered.

The boy managed to stay motionless for ten long minutes, even when a brown horn fly buzzed threateningly around his head. He knew a true woodsman had to learn patience, but it was a stern test.

At last Slim crept cautiously on for a few yards. He reached a spot where he could see through the brush to the next bend of the stream. He lay there a full minute, then gestured slowly to Jeff to follow him. The birds were still quiet.

Silently the boy crawled on till he lay close to Slim's elbow. Ahead, between the tree trunks he caught a glimpse of movement. Then he saw them—a big buck and a doe at the edge of the creek not fifty yards away.

"You take the she-'un," Slim breathed in his ear. They leveled their rifles and pulled back the hammers. At the double click of metal both deer lifted their heads, more curious than alarmed. Then the guns barked together.

The buck leaped high and fell where he was. Jeff had aimed at the doe's heart, but she must have moved at the instant he fired. Now she went floundering desperately up the bank and into the woods. Without stopping to reload, he raced after her, sure she was wounded.

Where the deer had gone through the brush, the twigs and leaves were splashed with bright red gouts of blood. Yet she kept on.

Jeff took no note of landmarks or of time. He was possessed by the single idea of overtaking his quarry, and he ran his hardest, listening to the crash of her progress ahead. Finally, after an endless time, his wind gave out and he stumbled over a fallen log, unable to get up. As he lay there gasping, he realized that he could no longer hear any sound from the woods around him. He staggered up, looking for the telltale blood drops, but none were to be seen.

His first thought was one of disgust that he had lost the deer. Then he thought of her blind terror and the agony she must be suffering and wished he had never fired at all. When he caught his breath, he reloaded the rifle. Doggedly he set about searching for the trail once more. His duty was to find the doe if he could and put her out of her misery.

After a while he realized that he had no idea where he

was. He must have run close to a mile, but whether the creek lay to his right or left or behind him he didn't know. He was about to fire his gun in the air in the hope that Slim would hear it when he caught the sound of a cheerful whistle.

The tall old man came out of the woods and stood there grinning at him. "Wal, hoss," he drawled, "looks like ye'd got yerself lost. Couldn't ketch up with the doe, either, could ye?"

Jeff kicked the dirt with his moccasin toe and hung his head in shame.

"Don't take it too hard," Slim told him. "She's back yonder, dead. Ye must ha' run right past her. 'Twa'n't a bit o' trouble findin' ye, though. The pair o'ye left a trail I could ha' follered blindfold."

The deer, when Jeff reached her, was lying in a thicket, her neck stretched out and her big eyes beginning to glaze.

"Mule deer," said Slim. "Look at them long ears, an' the black tail. They're some bigger'n a ordinary white-tail deer. See whar ye hit her? Smashed the shoulder. Must ha' run all this way on three legs. We'll skin her out an' I'll help ye carry the meat back."

When they returned to camp, loaded with venison, Slim praised Jeff's marksmanship and made no reference to his getting lost. For that the boy was grateful, but he made an inward resolve never to get into such a predicament again.

Two days after they left Deer Creek the course of the Platte changed direction, and they followed its windings toward the southwest.

"We'll come to the Sweetwater before very long," Jeff's father told him. "From there the trip gets tougher. Have to push along or we might get caught by an early snow in the mountains."

Jeff had been far too busy to do much drawing, except for a few hasty sketches he had made on scraps of paper he had brought. He was storing up pictures in his mind, however. The Crow hunters galloping among the buffalo—Chief White Calf in his full regalia—the towering mass of the Red Buttes above the river—all these were things he meant to paint, once he had some leisure. Lacking any canvas, he had carefully scraped the skin of the doe he had shot. He was planning to tan it later and use it as a surface for his pictures.

For two weeks they had seen no buffalo. Now, just above the Sweetwater, they came on countless thousands of them. As far as his eye could see, Jeff looked off across a plain that was black with the great shaggy beasts. And even beyond his vision, clouds of dust rose in the sky from the movement of still other herds.

The grass was gone, gnawed down to its roots. John Barlow looked worried. "Nothing left for the horses," he said. "We'll have to keep pushing till we're past 'em—unless they go on forever. And we'd better keep an eye peeled for Shoshones, too. They don't have many buffalo west of the divide, so they sometimes come over this way to get meat."

"Don't fergit the Blackfeet," Slim put in. "I know it's out o' their reg'lar country, but if huntin's been pore up north, they might show up regardless."

With these possibilities in mind, they kept going until after dark and made a cold camp, not risking a fire. A supper of river water and dried strips of venison seemed to Jeff to be poor rations for standing watch. However, he took his turn and stayed alert. Tomorrow, his father had promised, one of them would go out and get some buffalo meat while the others kept on the move.

As it turned out, there was no need to hunt. While they were breaking camp, just after dawn, a dozen buffalo came scrambling down the steep bluff to drink at the river. They were just out of range. But Jeff, already in the saddle, kicked his pony into action and dashed toward them without waiting for orders. He had almost reached the little herd and was picking his target when a young bull swung toward him and charged, horns lowered.

The buckskin side-stepped neatly and darted around to the bull's left side. Jeff decided the pony knew what was expected of his rider. Before the buffalo could wheel again, he drew a bead on the heart patch and fired.

Slim appeared beside him as he was dismounting by the fallen bull. Expertly the old hunter slit its throat and held a pan for the blood.

"Won't be quite as tasty as a fat cow," he said. "But this 'un's young enough to make decent eatin'. That hoss o' yourn, he really shines. Reckon he figgered if a buffler was goin' to come roarin' at him, somebody'd better teach the critter manners."

They feasted that night. Even the horses were able to eat again, for Pete LeBlanc found some sweet cottonwood trees by the river and stripped off armfuls of the tender bark to feed them. "Dat stuff," he explained, "she's mos' good as grass. In winter tam dat's how hoss keep alive."

* * * *

Two days later they left the buffalo behind. A stream called Sage Hen Creek came tumbling down out of the Granite Mountains, and in the canyon bottom where it flowed into the Sweetwater they found grass once more. It was too good a chance to miss. They remained there a day to put some flesh on the ponies, for there would be hard going ahead. At the same time John Barlow and Slim rode a mile or so up the canyon to the place where they had cached their traps in the spring. They brought them back to camp, safe and in good condition.

In the evening the three older men took counsel about their route. LeBlanc was for keeping on toward the South Pass and swinging north before they reached it. He said he knew some beaver country around the headwaters of the Popo Agie, if it hadn't been trapped out.

Jeff's father had a different idea. "Let's find our own country," he said. "Some place where nobody's ever been before. There must be dozens of hidden valleys 'twixt here and the Grand Teton."

"Yup," Slim agreed. "A few, anyhow. Tell ye what—I figger thar's one sech place I could find. Back in the fall o' twenty-three I was up on the Wind River, trappin' alone. That's whar my nickname come from, 'cause I used to call her my country. I was makin' a good ketch an' watchin' the plew pile up when along comes a bunch o' Blackfeet. They was mostly Dogs—young bucks that hadn't taken any scalps an' was out fer glory. They run off my three hosses, took all the fur, an' would ha' lifted my ha'r sure if I hadn't outsmarted 'em."

He lighted his pipe and took a couple of deep pulls before continuing. "A week or so before," he went on at last, "I'd dug myself a cache, whar I'd planned to hide the fur if'n I had to. When I seen thar was too many of 'em to shoot, I snuck in the cache an' pulled brush over the hole. They whooped an' hollered around fer a spell, an' then I guess they figgered I must be off somewhars on my trap line. Anyhow, come night, I crawled out an' hit fer the hills, travelin' over rocks, so's not to leave no trail.

"I was headed southwest. All I had was my rifle an' a leetle powder an' ball, an' the first day I was skeert to do any shootin' fer fear the Injuns'd hear it. Reckon I'd gone thirty mile afoot by the time I got so hongry I didn't keer. Then I managed to shoot me a bighorn sheep. Built a leetle fire in a box canyon an' et till I was like to bust.

"Wal, what I set out to tell ye was that on the third day I come to a river—the second one I'd had to cross. I didn't know it then, but it must ha' been the Popo Agie. I scouted along the bank till I found a shallow place an' went over. T'other side was a steep cliff. The stream was flowin' northeast, an' I figgered it'd jest take me back to the Wind River again, so I clumb up that cliff. It took me hours, an' I'll never know how I made it. But on t'other side was the purtiest valley I'd ever seed. Four or five mile wide, she was, an' all grass an' trees. Thar was a stream flowin' through—or would ha' been, 'cept fer the beaver dams. The cuttin's was everywhar. Jest guessin', I'd say thar must ha' been fifty thousan' beaver in that valley!

"With no traps to ketch 'em, I had to leave the place an' keep goin'. I follered up the stream a ways, clumb another cliff over the south rim, an' walked forty mile or so through dry country till I finally hit the Sweetwater. By luck thar was a passel o' trappers camped nigh to whar I come out, an' I went downriver with 'em in their bullboats."

"Golly!" said Jeff. "Forty mile afoot, an' no water! You must ha' been about finished 'fore you made it, Slim."

The old man grinned. "Mebbe a mite tired," he admitted. "But I was younger then—tough as a grizzly. I'd filled my canteen 'fore I set out, so 'twa'n't too bad. Near as I kin recollec', the place whar I come out was only a day or so upriver from here."

John Barlow got up and stirred the fire. "For once, old-timer, I'm inclined to think you're telling the truth," he said with a grin. "If you can find that trail north from the Sweetwater, I'd be willing to try it. How about you, Pete?"

The Frenchman nodded dubiously. "She soun' good," he replied, "all but dose Injun. Mebbe dey come back, huh?"

" 'Tain't likely," Slim reassured him. "That was four-five year back, an' it had been a bad buffler season. This place I been tellin' ye about is a long way from Blackfoot country, an' they'd never git into it from the north—not on hosses, anyhow."

To Jeff, of course, the idea of leaving the beaten track and striking off into unexplored country was an exciting prospect. He tried to picture Slim's lost valley as he lay in his blanket that night. Mountains he could understand, and streams and forests. The part he found harder to imagine was the rich trapping, for he knew little about beaver or their habits.

His father was gone when he woke next morning, but he returned inside of an hour with a blacktail buck. They ate the tender parts for breakfast, then spent most of the day drying and smoking meat to take on their journey. The horses grazed happily in the lush grass beside the river. Men and beasts alike were well fed and rested by the time they started out the following morning.

They moved steadily along the rough trail beside the river. Sometimes it climbed on twisting, narrow ledges. In other places it ran close to the stream and among the cottonwoods that lined the bank. Slim rode in the lead, stopping now and then to study the landmarks.

It was nearly sundown when he pulled up and pointed to the rocky slope at the right.

"That's whar I come down," he called. "An' the fellers in the bullboats had hauled out an' camped right about here. Mus' be a better way to git up thar, though. I recollec' I nigh broke my neck comin' down."

"I don't wonder," Jeff's father answered. "It would take a goat to climb that cliff. Let's make camp, anyhow, and before dark I'll scout ahead for an easier place to go up."

He rode off while the others were unloading the pack horses and getting supper. At twilight he returned with the news that there was a break in the cliffs a couple of miles up the river.

"I reckon the horses can make it," he said. "Only we may have to climb afoot and lead 'em up."

At daybreak they breakfasted, filled their canteens, watered the stock, and resaddled. Half an hour later they were struggling up the rocky side of the gorge. John Barlow led the way, doubling back and forth on yard-wide ledges, scrambling over treacherous rockslides, and dragging his unwilling pony after him. The pack animals were roped together and followed obediently where the men and the saddle horses led.

The ascent took more than an hour, but they finally reached the top without accident. There they stopped to get their breath and look around them.

Jeff saw a lofty plateau stretching away and away to a distant range of white-peaked mountains. Except for a few clumps of dusty sage it was barren of all vegetation. And no living thing moved on the rolling plain. Not even a jack rabbit was to be seen.

Slim took his bearings by the sun. "We head due north from here," he said. "Have to keep movin' steady but don't take it too fast. Like I told ye, it's a good forty mile."

chapter 7

That journey across the high, arid plain was an experience Jeff would remember for a long time. By midmorning the sun beat on them with a searing brightness, reflected back by the white patches of alkali. There was no shade, no way to escape the glare. The boy slouched listlessly in his saddle, the sweat pouring off his body and drying quickly in the heat. Dust rose from under the plodding hoofs, stinging Jeff's eyes and tasting bitter in his mouth.

He was constantly tempted to drink from his canteen, but his father had laid down the law before they started. He could have only one good swig at noon and another in the evening.

"If you go a little thirsty today," he warned Jeff, "you may have enough water to keep you alive through tomorrow—or however long it takes us to get to a creek or a spring."

The ponies suffered even more than their riders. They went at a walk, heads drooping, eyes half closed against the dust. By afternoon they had gaunted down till their ribs were showing. Jeff wondered if the buckskin's thoughts, like his own, were on fresh, clear water and green grass and shade.

It was about four o'clock when he looked ahead, gasped once, and let out a dry-throated yell.

"Water!" he cried. "A whole grove o' trees—and a pond! Not more'n half a mile away!"

He was urging his pony to a trot when his father held up a hand to restrain him. "That's what it looks like," he told the boy. "But it's only a mirage. There's nothing really there. You'll see in a minute."

Unbelieving, Jeff kept his eyes on the green and lovely grove. Even as he looked, the trees seemed to stretch taller, then gradually fade away. Within thirty seconds there was nothing before him but the desert, hot and empty.

Slim rode up beside him chuckling. " 'Nough to turn a feller's wits, ain't it?" he asked. "Ye'd ha' swore to what ye see on a stack o' Bibles—an' then it's all gone."

"But," Jeff asked in puzzled wonder, "what makes it happen?"

"Somethin' about the light, so they tell me," the old mountain man replied. "Ask yore paw—he's eddicated."

That night, when they had eaten their jerked venison and washed it down with a skimpy drink of water, Jeff tried to get an answer from his father.

"A mirage is pretty tough to explain," he said, "unless you've studied natural science. Light is refracted when it passes through air of different densities. Up here, where the sun heats the air, it rises and expands, and you get an overhead layer that bends the light rays. What we saw was a sure enough grove of trees and some water. But they may be a long way off—clear over the horizon, somewhere. It was the refraction that made 'em seem so close."

Jeff was a long way from understanding, but he had to be satisfied. The night turned chill after the sun had set, and he slept with his blanket wrapped tightly around him. He missed the noises he had heard along the river—the lapping of water on the shore, the munching sound of grazing horses, the howl of a hunting coyote. Here there was only the steady rush of the wind.

At dawn they rose, shivering, drank a little from the canteens, and pushed onward. The horses, weak from lack of food and water, went slowly, their dry tongues hanging from their mouths. Far overhead the boy saw three or four buzzards wheeling on the air currents, and he squirmed at the sight. The birds were waiting, he knew, for a man or an animal to die.

Pete saw them too, and crossed himself. Slim merely laughed. "Don't worry, boys," he croaked. "We're goin' to fool 'em. Keep yer chin up an' remember we're more'n halfway across."

He had calculated right. A little before noon the scorched plain began to slope gradually downward. Suddenly Jeff's buckskin whinnied and pricked up his ears, and in a moment they were all moving at a faster gait.

"They've scented water," John Barlow said through parched lips. "Have to hold 'em, or they'll bolt right over when we get to the rim."

By the time they reached it, however, the rim proved to be not a cliff edge but a slope no steeper than a barn roof. Slim led the way, picking a trail of sorts down the ledges and broken rock. And Jeff, following him, stared ahead into the valley. After what they had come through, it seemed to him the loveliest place he had ever seen. A stream glinted in the sun, winding through thick green grass and trees, mile after mile. Far away to the north the valley ended at the base of a mountain range. Forest covered the lower slopes, but the peaks were naked rock and snow.

"Wagh!" Slim cried in satisfaction. "Thar she be! What did this coon tell ye? The Garden of Eden couldn't ha' been no purtier!"

"For once, old-timer," John Barlow said with a chuckle,

"you're dead right. Everything you said was true. I can count a dozen beaver ponds from here, and look yonder! Those dark specks on the meadow—they're buffalo by thunder!"

On the gentler slope below the rocks the horses broke into a trot, then an eager canter. The cavalcade passed through the fringe of woods that half hid the creek and came out on a grassy meadow close to the bank. In a moment the ponies stood knee-deep, their muzzles buried in clear, cool water.

"Careful, boys—don't let 'em drink too much at first," John Barlow warned.

The animals kicked and struggled but were finally pulled back out of the stream. As soon as the saddles and packs were taken off, they rolled in the cool grass and began to feed hungrily.

Meanwhile, the trappers stripped off their dust-caked clothes and plunged into the creek, splashing and swimming like a crowd of ten-year-olds. Afterward they lay naked on the bank and let the sun dry them.

Slim stretched his long, wiry arms and grunted happily. "This hoss is hongry," he announced. "But I don't aim to eat jerky again fer a spell. How 'bout you an' me makin' a hunt, Jeff?"

John Barlow looked at his son's eager face and nodded. "Good idea," he said. "Pete and I'll be looking around for a place to build the cabins."

The hunters went afoot, giving the horses a rest. Slim led the way down the little river. He pointed to beaver cuttings along the shore, where the busy animals had felled aspens for food and for dam-building. The marks of the big chisel-like teeth were plain to be seen on the stumps. Then they came to a pond, where they saw a score of domed lodges made of sticks and mud, each built, so Slim told the boy, with an underwater entrance. Jeff wondered where the beaver were. He was about to ask when his companion pointed to a sleek brown head moving rapidly out from shore. The beaver caught a glimpse of them, slapped the water loudly with its tail, and dived out of sight.

"Look," said the mountain man, "yonder's a couple more big fellers, cuttin' down aspens. They've got front teeth that are sharp as chisels. Anyhow, it looks like thar's plenty of 'em."

They had traveled perhaps a mile when Slim held up his hand and stood listening. The creek made a sharp bend just beyond. After a moment the old hunter beckoned to Jeff to follow him quietly. They crept in among the trees and cut across till they could see the stream beyond the bend.

"Elk!" Slim whispered. "Two of 'em down thar drinkin'."

With the greatest caution they crawled forward till the big animals were in plain view through the screening brush—a young, antlered bull and a cow, some fifty yards away.

"Take the cow," Slim breathed. "I'll try fer the bull. Don't cock the hammer till ye've got her in yer sights."

Jeff braced his left elbow on his knee for a steadier aim, lined up the rifle on the cow elk's side, and glanced at his companion.

"Now!" Slim whispered. Together they cocked their rifles and fired. At the double report both elk jumped, but the bull fell where he was, knee-deep in the stream. The cow bounded a few yards up the bank, staggered, and dropped.

"Good shootin'," said Slim. "Only reason the he-'un went down fust, I was usin' a buffler gun. Wal, we got us all the meat we kin handle fer a spell, I reckon."

Jeff helped him drag the bull out on shore, and together they skinned the animals.

"Elk hide makes the best moccasins fer winter," Slim told him. "It's heavier'n deerskin an' wears longer. The meat's full as good as venison, too—an' thar's twice as much of it. Looks like we'll be eatin' high on the hawg this winter."

Jeff went back to camp and got a pony to pack in the meat. His father didn't seem surprised when he announced their good luck.

"I could see there was plenty o' game around," he said. "Next thing is to get a roof over us, so we can start trapping when the fur's ready."

Before nightfall they had thrown together a pole lean-to and thatched it with fir boughs. That would give them temporary shelter until cabins could be built. John Barlow had picked a good campsite on a knoll in the woods, facing the creek. The next morning they all took their axes and set to work felling logs, cutting them to twelve-foot lengths, and notching the ends so that they would fit snugly together. The first cabin was finished in a day and a half, and Jeff and his father moved in.

After months of sleeping outdoors on the ground, the crude log shack seemed almost luxurious to Jeff. It had a low doorway and one small opening that served as a window. There was no chimney, but a smoke hole in the roof worked well enough. Later, before winter came, they would chink the logs with mud to keep out the snow and keep a fire going on the clay floor. Their rough-hewn bunks were filled with fir boughs, soft and springy.

Slim and Pete were in less of a hurry to get their cabin built. The Frenchman wanted, first of all, to put in some traps and start catching beaver. He had packed his traps all the way from St. Louis. Now he was anxious to use them, even though he knew the fur wouldn't be prime for several more weeks. Slim's interest lay in exploration. He set off on his pony and was away for two days, riding into every corner of the valley. His eyes were shining when he returned.

"Funny thing, Jawn," he told Jeff's father after supper. "I'd like to bet no Injuns have ever found this place. Down at the north end she butts up agin' a solid wall o' rock—cliffs half a mile high, 'pears like. The creek jest drops off into a hole an' flows out under the mountain! That means no stray Blackfeet would find it, comin' from the north. An' that alkali plain we crossed would sure discourage any Crows from the east or Snakes from the west an' south."

Barlow nodded. "Makes sense," he said, "but that's no reason to get careless. After all, *we* found it, didn't we?"

The next day it was Jeff's turn to go with his father and look over the country. It was all that Slim had said and more. In a ride of twenty miles they counted nearly a hundred beaver dams. But in Jeff's case it was the beauty of the valley itself that made the deepest impression. Back from the stream there were green meadows dotted with flowers of many colors, and around them rose the woods. There were fir and lodgepole pine climbing the hillsides, cottonwood and quaking asp in the lowlands.

Halfway down the valley they came to a long stretch of parklike grazing land and saw little groups of buffalo roaming in the distance. Jeff wanted to shoot one, but his father restrained him.

"We're in no need of meat," he said. "And unless I miss my guess, this herd won't leave the valley. They've got prime grass now and a fair place to winter, and it doesn't look as if they'd been hunted. So if we're careful not to stampede 'em, we'll have our supply o' meat right here on the hoof."

As they rode on, other creatures made their appearance. High up on the rocky slope to their left, Jeff saw three or four grayish-brown animals moving across the cliff face. They were nearly a mile away, but in the clear air he could tell that they weren't deer or elk. Then, as one of them turned its head, he caught a glimpse of great curling horns. He was looking at his first bighorn ram—a "cimarron," as the mountain men called the wild sheep of the Rockies.

In one place the beaver had dammed up a real lake, nearly half a mile long, with a marshy area at the upper end. As they rode past, a flock of ducks went up with whirring wings. And out in the middle of the lake a loon called. The echo of its crazy laughter came back weirdly from the canyon walls.

At the foot of the valley they sat their horses and stared at the vanishing stream. There was a dark, jagged hole under the cliffs, and the water went boiling over a fall to disappear into the natural tunnel.

"Slim was right," Barlow commented. "No Indians are likely to find their way in from this end. I wonder where the creek goes to. Probably it comes gushing out o' the ground in a big spring, miles away on the other side o' the mountain."

They dismounted beside the waterfall, ate some dried elk meat, and boiled tea over a little fire. In the afternoon they rode back, studying the course of the stream for good trapping places. The sun was close to the western peaks as they neared camp. Suddenly Jeff's pony gave a snort and a shiver. On the other side of the creek the boy saw a monstrous gray shape lumbering out of the water. It was a bear, infinitely bigger than anything he had imagined. The grizzly shook itself, turned toward them, and rose majestically on its hind legs, standing a good eight feet tall. Its nostrils quivered as it sniffed the strange scent, and it stood with huge forearms hanging comically across its pale paunch.

"Silvertip," Jeff's father said quietly. "What Slim calls a 'white bear.' Mostly they'll leave you alone if you don't bother 'em. But they're sometimes partial to horse meat. I hope this fellow stays on his own side o' the river."

As yet they had no corral, but that night they hobbled the ponies and took turns standing horse-guard. Jeff had the first watch, from dusk to a little before midnight. While the older men smoked their pipes around the dying campfire, he sat on a stump with his rifle and kept an eye on the horses. One or two of them seemed a little restless, but gradually they all grew quiet and lay down peacefully enough.

The last pink glow was gone from the peaks and the valley floor lay in the black of night. Then the moon rose. It silvered the snow of the mountains and glinted softly on the water. The shadows it cast in the clearing seemed to move as the breeze stirred the aspen leaves. Jeff shifted his weight on the stump and took a firmer grip on his rifle. He remembered the giant grizzly too vividly to feel sleepy. Yet he didn't want to act like a tenderfoot in his nervousness.

Then one of the horses snorted and heaved to its feet. It was his own buckskin. It stood only twenty yards from him, and in the moonlight he could see the quiver of its flanks, the flare of its nostrils. From the edge of the woods appeared a moving shadow, huge and bulky and frosted with silver where the moon touched it.

chapter 8

All the horses were up now, tugging at their hobbles and squealing with fear. Jeff ran toward them, and as he ran, he yelled for help at the top of his lungs. The cry stopped the grizzly for a second or two. Then it came on again at a shambling trot.

The bear was only a few yards from the huddled horses when Jeff fired. His hands were shaking with terror and excitement, but he took aim as best he could and pulled the trigger. His bullet must have struck the big beast somewhere in the chest. It gave a roar of rage and pain and charged the floundering horses. With one stroke of a mighty paw it crushed the head of the nearest pony.

Jeff was trying frantically to reload when a tall figure sprang past him. It was his father, hurrying to the rescue. John Barlow was only ten paces from the wounded bear when he fired. At the blast of the heavy Hawken rifle the grizzly reared up to its full height, gave one choking snarl, and toppled to the ground with a crash like a falling tree.

"Keep away from him!" Jeff's father panted. "He may not be dead yet."

To make certain, he loaded his gun again, approached

the furry monster cautiously, and sent a bullet smashing into the brain at point-blank range. Meanwhile, the other two men had arrived. With them Jeff hurried to the ponies. The one that had been killed was a pack horse—not the buckskin as he had feared. But all the rest were in pitiable condition, maddened by fright. Some had tangled their legs in the hobbles and thrown themselves. Others were kicking and biting, trying to break away. It took a full half hour to calm them down.

Slim supervised the skinning of the bear, but when it came to turning over the half-ton carcass, all four of them had to lend a hand.

"Ye hit him, fair enough," the old mountain man told Jeff. "Right yere—close to the heart. But with that light gun it was like prickin' him with a pin. Jest made him twicet as mad. Yer paw's first bullet went through the throat an' busted his spine. It takes a powerful shot to knock out a big white b'ar, an' this yere's a big 'un—no mistake about it."

When they spread out the immense hide, it measured more than eight feet long and nearly as wide. The head, with its great, grinning teeth, had been left on. The claws were as long as a man's fingers.

Even though he had failed to kill the grizzly, Jeff felt that the huge skin was partly his trophy. "We can spread it on the floor o' the cabin," he told his father. "Give us a nice warm rug to walk on when the weather gets cold."

The bear was fat with summer feeding, and Slim saved a large pile of the fat to try out for grease. "It's fine fer fryin'," he said, "an' good fer wounds an' scratches, too. Or ye kin use it to slick down yer ha'r like the Injuns do. The meat ain't much to brag about—only the paws. They're gen'ally sweet an' tender."

It was close to midnight when Jeff finally got to sleep.

The others continued to stand watch, but there was no further trouble that night.

After breakfast Pete lashed the buffalo-skin bag that held his traps on the back of a pack pony and went off down the creek.

Slim stretched his arms and looked after the departing Frenchman with a grin. "Let him work hisself to death fer pore pelts," he told Jeff. "This child has et meat long enough to crave suthin' different. Let's you an' me ketch us a fish."

They took hooks and lines from the bundle of trade goods, dug some grubs from under a fallen log to use for bait, and set off along the stream. Jeff found a shaded pool below a riffle and dropped his bait on the surface, letting it float down. Instantly he saw a commotion in the pool and two big trout struck almost at the same time. There was a struggle for the prize, but one of the fish got the hook in its mouth and swallowed it whole. Chuckling, Jeff hauled it out, flopping, on the bank. He had to use his knife to free the hook, but as soon as he rebaited, he caught a second trout and then a third. All of them were huge by Illinois standards. He judged they would weigh three or four pounds apiece.

When he carried them back to camp, he found Slim had made a similar haul. They cleaned and fried them in bear's grease for their noon meal, and Jeff had to agree that trout made a delicious change from a steady diet of venison and buffalo meat.

* * * *

For several lazy days they fished and hunted and explored their valley. Then one night the wind came sharp out of the north and the temperature dropped. By morning Jeff found a white coating of frost on the grass. His breath was cloudy in the cold air. The first sharp bite of autumn had come.

"All right, son," his father told him. "Time to start getting ready. Weather like this'll thicken the beaver fur up fast."

Jeff was surprised to see that in spite of the cold his father came out and sat in front of the shack bare-legged, in nothing but his hunting shirt. He was cutting away the lower part of his buckskin leggings with a knife.

"We'll be in the water up to our knees a lot o' the time," he explained. "Buckskin stretches too much when it's wet an' shrinks too tight afterward, when it dries. You'll be all right because you've still got your cloth pants. Slim and I'll have to sew cloth on the bottoms of ours. Fetch me my possible sack and I'll show you."

From the buckskin bag he took his awl and a length of supple deer sinew. With these he made a workmanlike job of sewing a piece of heavy cotton drill to each leg of the buckskin breeches from the knee down. When he had them on, he reached into the possible sack once more.

"Now this," he told the boy, "is about the most important thing in catching beaver."

He held up a small bottle made from the tip of an antelope horn, scraped thin enough to see through, and carefully stoppered. Inside Jeff could see a brownish liquid.

"It's what they call 'castrum,' " his father went on. "Slim and I made it last winter out o' the castor glands from beaver carcasses. We bait our traps with a drop or two o' the stuff, and it makes the beaver come like an old toper after a bottle. This'll be enough to start us off, and as soon as we begin catching 'em, we can make plenty more."

They laid out the traps that day, scrubbing away the rust and putting a little grease on the springs and triggers to make sure they would snap shut at a touch on the pan. Each trap had a thin five-foot chain attached to it.

"We'll set your line on the upstream side," Jeff's father said. "There are three or four ponds to work, so you shouldn't run out o' beaver for a month, anyhow. Take the ax out now and cut a bundle o' stakes. You sharpen one end so it'll go down in the mud—and make sure they're long enough. Six or seven feet at least."

Before supper Jeff was back with about twenty stakes, cut from stout aspen saplings. John Barlow looked them over approvingly. "Good enough," he said. "We'll be ready to start, come daylight."

It was a cold night, with more frost at dawn. Most of the leaves had started to turn yellow on the quaking asps. The horses got up stiffly and stood hunched and shivering until the sun broke over the eastern rim.

Jeff and his father finished breakfast, tied the boy's ten traps and the stakes on the back of a pack pony, and started up the creek bank. A quarter of a mile from camp they came to the first mud-and-stick beaver dam.

Barlow beckoned to his son to follow and stepped into the shallow water. As they waded up along the shore, he pointed out the likely spots to set traps. One was a slide—a smooth, steep path in the clay, used by beaver to put logs in the pond. Another was a trail leading up to a fresh cutting among the aspens. And in a number of places there were beaver lodges with underwater doorways not too far from the bank.

When their survey was completed, Jeff slung four traps over his shoulder and watched his father make the first set. He opened the jaws and adjusted the trigger carefully. Then he placed the trap in about a foot and a half of water in front of one of the cutting trails. Around it, bent above the pan, he stuck thin shoots, the upper tips of which he had dipped in the castrum horn. Jeff sniffed at the stuff and made a face. It might be alluring to beaver, but it had an odd, unpleasant smell to a human.

The next part of the operation was to fasten a stake to the end of the chain and plant it as far out from shore as it would reach.

"The thing you don't want," John Barlow explained, "is to have your beaver haul the trap out on the bank. He'll gnaw off his leg and get away unless he's kept in deep water."

The second trap was placed in front of one of the dens. Here the bottom dropped off too steeply to set a stake, and Barlow fastened the chain to a short log—a "float-stick" as the trappers called it.

By noonday they had set all ten traps along the edges of the two nearest ponds. Later, Jeff went with his father to a place farther down the valley where he established his own trap line. On the way home, at sunset, they encountered Slim riding along the shore.

"Wagh!" cried the old mountain man. "Look yere, boys!"

He pointed to a big, dark bundle across his pony's rump. "Buffler!" he said. "Purtiest young cow y'ever seed. Got yer traps all set? Me, too. Reckon we're in business."

They feasted on liver, tongue, and hump meat that night, and Jeff rolled up in his blankets almost too full to move. When he woke in the shivery chill before sunrise, however, he was ready and eager for the day's work. He could hardly wait to eat breakfast before going to see what was in his traps.

He took his rifle, mounted the buckskin pony, and set out. The very first trap yielded a full-grown beaver. The animal had drowned trying to reach shore—a tragic end that gave Jeff a pang of remorse. But he had come to the mountains to catch fur, and if he wanted to become a successful trapper, he knew he would have to get used to such things. Opening the trap, he put the dripping beaver in a big burlap bag and slung it across his saddle.

Then he reset the steel jaws and left the trap in the same spot, putting fresh lure on the aspen switches.

The second trap was gone. He looked about for the float stick and finally saw it under the surface, wedged across the opening to the beaver lodge. When he hauled on the chain, he succeeded in recovering the trap. It had been sprung all right, but all he found in it was a set of beaver toes, cut away just above the grip of the jaws. He hoped the maimed animal would recover.

There seemed to be no point in resetting the trap there, so he found a fresh place, a little farther up. By the time he had the trap in position the icy water had numbed his legs to the knees. He ran back and forth on the bank, stamping his feet till the circulation came back.

When the sun stood overhead, proclaiming it was noon, Jeff had visited all ten of his traps. From them he had taken a total of six fine beaver. They weighed from thirty to forty pounds apiece, and at the end the bulging sack across the saddle was too heavy for him to lift. He walked the two miles back to camp, leading the buckskin, and it was a proud moment when he came in sight of the cook fire and hailed the others.

"Hey!" he called. "I got six of 'em!"

Pete LeBlanc grinned and nodded. "By gar!" he said. "Dat's plenty fine!"

His father made no comment, though Jeff could see he was pleased. Slim puffed at his pipe and shook his head. "Ain't that jest what ye'd expect a tenderfoot to do?" he asked plaintively. "Beginners is allus plumb shot with luck."

As the boy soon learned, however, his day's catch was not at all remarkable. Slim had taken nine beaver and his father eight. Pete hadn't covered all of his line but had brought in five so far.

They spent most of the afternoon skinning out the fur.

John Barlow showed Jeff how it was done, and after some trouble with the first one he managed to get all the pelts off. Then they had to be sewn on hoops made of springy saplings, and fleshed. This last was a long and tiresome job, for every particle of fat must be scraped away with a fleshing knife. Finally the skins, on their stretchers, were set up in rows to dry in the sun. Before bedtime that night, Jeff had begun to realize that the trade of a trapper wasn't all romance and high adventure.

chapter 9

The crisp fall weather held for more than a week. Then their activities were interrupted by a two-day rainstorm. At least it was rain there in the valley. Higher, among the peaks, the snow was drifting. When the sky finally cleared and the sun came out, they saw the rocky walls gleaming white clear down to the timber line.

The elk had come down out of the high meadows, now packed with snow, and grazed in the bottoms along the stream. From dawn to dark the cliff walls echoed with the loud, bugle-like challenges of the bulls, for this was the rutting season and they were eager for battle.

"No sense tanglin' with a bull elk when he's feelin' ornery as that," Slim told Jeff. "If'n ye want meat, jest wait fer a good shot at a cow."

It was only a day or two later that the boy was a spectator at one of the most thrilling fights he had ever seen. He was wading along the shore of the second pond, visiting his traps, when he caught a glimpse of five elk among the trees only a hundred yards away. Four of them were cows. The fifth, a big bull with antlers like a rocking chair, strode out in front of his harem and gave his trumpet call so loud that Jeff thought for a moment the challenge was directed at himself.

Quickly the answer came back. Another bull, young and proud, trotted out from the aspens. He was alone—a bachelor looking for a mate. The two males faced each other, snorting and pawing at the ground. Their great racks of horns came together with a clash like breaking crockery, and they pushed and strained and grunted till the older bull's weight began to count. The other gave ground a step at a time, then pulled free and sprang nimbly aside.

Jeff's sympathies were with the younger elk. "Hit him again, quick!" he muttered. And before the words were out of his mouth, the lighter bull charged, this time from the side. Unable to turn in time, the big fellow was nearly knocked off his feet. He squawled with rage and swung back to face his adversary. But Jeff could see blood welling from his shoulder, where a sharp antler tip had pierced the hide.

Once more the fiery youngster charged, but this time the big bull was ready for him. Their horns locked, and the heaving and straining began again. The lighter animal angled sidewise till his feet were on higher ground, and with this advantage he forced his opponent backward yard by yard. The old bull was a veteran of many fights, but the wound had weakened him. He was panting hard now. After a minute or two of valiant struggle he gave up and broke away. At a lurching gallop he left the field to his conqueror.

Jeff felt a little sorry for the beaten champion, but when he saw that two of the cows followed their former lord, he knew his pity was wasted. The young bull lifted his head in a bugle call of triumph, then pranced over to the two remaining females and led them off down the valley. Jeff watched till they were out of sight, then went back to his traps.

It was amazing how fast the pelts piled up. In the last three weeks of October they took more than four hundred beaver amongst them. As he gained in experience, Jeff was catching almost as many as the others. On one record day he brought in ten—a beaver for every trap. That evening he was working by firelight late into the night before he finished fleshing the skins.

As the weather grew colder, there was often a skim of ice along the creek bank in the mornings. Wading in that freezing water was a painful business, and Jeff finally made himself an oversize pair of moccasins. Into them he was able to stuff double layers of blanket cloth, wrapped around his feet. And though his legs still grew numb at times, he endured the cold and tried not to show it.

"Skins is dried," Slim remarked one night. "We better take time off to make up some packs."

Next morning they all turned to at the job. Jeff's part in it was to cut the thongs and take the pelts off their frames. Pete took each skin and folded it properly. And John Barlow and Slim did the baling. They used a press like a giant nutcracker, made from two logs tied with rawhide. With this contrivance a pile of skins was squeezed into a compact bundle and lashed with thongs. Each pack contained sixty beaver pelts and weighed roughly a hundred pounds.

"Better'n a hunderd an' ten plew," Slim commented when they had finished. "An' with luck we'll double that 'fore winter shets down."

Jeff did some mental arithmetic. At six dollars a plew, they had already earned between six hundred and fifty and seven hundred dollars! It seemed like a lot of money, even divided among the four of them.

Another incident that interrupted their trapping occurred a few days later. Along with the game that now thronged the floor of the valley, other animals had also arrived. Sometimes they saw big gray lobo wolves slinking through the woods. And one night Jeff was wakened by a sharp scream, like the cry of a woman in pain.

His father sat up in the bunk. "Mountain lion!" He answered Jeff's unspoken question. "What Slim calls a 'painter.' I'd better go out an' take a look at the horses."

He came in again a few moments later, took his rifle off the pegs on the wall, and told Jeff to put on his jacket. "They're fidgety," he said. "I reckon we'd better build up a good fire outside, so's to keep the varmint away."

Jeff collected a stack of wood and lighted the tinder with flint and steel. In a few minutes the logs were blazing high, and the hobbled ponies drew close to the fire for warmth and protection. John Barlow sat down with his back against a tree and sent Jeff back to bed in the cabin.

"I'll doze right here," he told the boy. "Come morning we'd better do something about building a corral."

After he was in his bunk Jeff heard the lion scream once more, but the sound seemed to come from some distance away, and he dropped off to sleep. At daybreak his father came in, stiff with cold.

"Time to rise an' shine," he said gruffly. "We've got a big day's work to do. Start a fire for breakfast. I'm going to talk to Slim and Pete."

By sunup they were all busy chopping poles, and before the day ended they had thrown together a fairly stout corral, big enough to hold all the ponies.

"I dunno," said Slim, looking at their handiwork. "That ol' painter kin likely climb or jump any sort o' fence. Wisht we had a good houn' dawg along. Then we could trail the critter an' git rid of him fer keeps."

At evening the sky had clouded over and the wind was blowing from the north. Jeff went to bed shivering, but with blankets and a buffalo robe to warm him, he was soon sleeping comfortably. It was a little after midnight when a commotion outside aroused him. By the dim light of the embers he could see his father reaching for his rifle. Jeff sprang up, got his own gun, and dashed out after him.

The horses were squealing with terror and crashing against the sides of their pen. A light snow had started to fall, and in the pitch darkness it was impossible to see what was happening. But in a moment there was a flash near the corral and the loud report of the Hawken gun.

"Did you get him, Pa?" Jeff shouted through chattering teeth.

"No," the reply came back. "Scared him off, though. We need some light out here. Fetch some coals and we'll start a fire."

When the boy returned with a shovelful of hot embers, his father piled dry branches together. As the flames flared up, Jeff could see the frightened ponies still milling about in the enclosure. One of them—Slim's roan—was bleeding badly from claw wounds on the shoulder and foreleg, and it wasn't until John Barlow roped him that they could get close enough to examine the damage.

About that time Pete and Slim came running up. The old mountain man was grim with anger at the attack on his horse. He swore fiercely under his breath as he rubbed the wound with bear's grease.

"I ain't goin' to tetch another trap," he announced, "till I've put a bullet through that varmint's black heart!"

The snow stopped falling a little while later, and when Jeff rose next morning, the sky was clear. On the ground lay an inch-deep layer of white. Hurrying out to the corral, he found clear-cut cougar tracks leading up to the fence, then away from it on the opposite side. The big cat had gone in long bounds, frightened off by the rifle. Slim was there looking at the tracks, too.

"This child figgers we kin read the critter's trail like a book," he said. "What say, boy? Want to come along?"

Nothing could have pleased Jeff more. He gobbled a few mouthfuls of breakfast, took his rifle, powder horn, and bullet pouch, and joined Slim at the other cabin.

The tracks were easy enough to follow for the first half mile. The cat had run some distance, stopped to look back, seen the fire, and gone on at a walk. After a while the trail led into thick brush where Slim cautioned Jeff to go warily.

"Might ha' holed up in here or clumb a tree," said the old trapper. "So better keep yer eyes peeled."

They found a place where the cougar had lain down briefly under a jack pine. Then the tracks left the thicket and angled uphill toward the rocky wall of the canyon. The snow on the ledges was beginning to melt in the sun, and Slim moved faster, afraid the pug marks would disappear. Soon they came to a spot where the animal had crouched, facing the valley. A few yards below, Jeff could see a deer path, and when he looked where Slim pointed he saw traces of blood down there in the snow.

"Critter done made a kill!" Slim exclaimed. "Likely a small doe he could lug away. We'd oughta git him now fer sure!"

They scrambled down off the ledge and hurried along the broad trail left by the dragging carcass of the deer. In another clump of brush, the mountain lion had stopped to feed. They found the mangled body of a half-grown fawn and many big cat tracks around it. Then the trail led directly toward the rocks.

After ten minutes of climbing the hunters came out on bare shale where no prints showed. Jeff looked around him, discouraged. "Guess we've lost him now," he said.

But Slim shook his head. "This hoss ain't givin' up. If'n you was a lion with a full meal in yer belly, what'd ye do? Go an' sleep it off. He's got him a den in these rocks—not too fur off, nuther, or I'm no jedge."

His keen old eyes searched the cliff. "Yon's a leetle cave," he whispered. "What say we take a look?"

They clambered higher and reached a narrow shelf that led to the cave mouth. Silently Slim pointed to something at the entrance, and Jeff's heart began to beat faster. It was the leg bone of some animal, cracked and gnawed clean. More than that, the boy was sure he had caught a whiff of rank cat smell.

Slim cocked his rifle. At the sound there came a low growl from the cave, only two or three yards away. Jeff, too, pulled back the hammer of his gun and they waited, scarcely breathing. The growling had ceased. Cautiously the old mountain man stooped, picked up a pebble, and tossed it into the cave. Before he could even straighten up, the huge cat leaped past in a tawny flash, landing among the rocks below.

Jeff whipped his rifle to his shoulder and took a quick shot, echoed an instant later by the bark of the heavier buffalo gun. They saw the cougar bound on for a dozen yards, then tumble and roll over, its claws ripping at the air.

"He's about done fer," said Slim. "But don't git close till yore gun's ready. These critters is like snakes—take a heap o' killin'."

They waited till both rifles were reloaded, then approached the long, furry body among the rocks. There was no need for another shot. Two bullet holes, one in the side just over the heart, the other through the head, guaranteed that the giant cat was dead.

"Either one of 'em would ha' stopped him," Slim commented. "You'd better go back fer a hoss while I start skinnin'. We'll eat real meat tonight. Like I allus said, painter steak's the best thar is."

They got the hide and the meat back to camp, then went to look at their traps, neglected the previous day. Jeff found

only three beaver in his, and had to break ice along the shore to bring them in. The other trappers had no more luck.

"It's getting toward the end o' the season," John Barlow said. "Another week and we're going to have to pull our traps if this cold weather holds."

He explained that as soon as thick ice formed on the ponds, nearly all the beaver would be snug in their dens. The cutting of winter food would have ended, and the aspen logs with their succulent bark would be stored away in deep water near the lodge entrances. None of the animals would appear again until spring.

"Some say they sleep all winter, same as a bear," he told Jeff. "Others think they stay awake and eat a little when they're hungry. I'd guess it's a little o' both. An old trapper told me once he'd chopped into a lodge in January and never found a beaver. The whole family'd swum out under the ice."

That night Jeff had his first taste of cougar meat. He was reluctant even to try it until he saw the others eating with apparent relish. After the first bite he knew they weren't pretending. The meat was sweet and tender, a little like veal but with a strange, wild flavor that was delicious.

The talk around the fire was of plans for the winter. Slim, Pete, and Barlow were all old winterers—*hivernants* as the French phrase went. They knew how to live through the bitter weather and the deep snow with nothing to help them but their axes and rifles. Jeff took confidence from them, and in a way he looked forward to the experience. Once they were settled in, he knew he would have time to do some drawing. A hundred vivid pictures were going through his head, and he itched to begin putting them into line and color.

Before that, however, he knew there were busy days

ahead. The cabins must be chinked and readied for winter. Big piles of firewood must be cut and a store of meat laid in. That meant hunting! Before he went to bed he cleaned and greased the old Kentucky rifle.

chapter 10

A brief spell of Indian summer weather enabled them to stretch the fur season out for another week. Then a hard freeze came, and they took up their traps. Counting the fresh pelts as well as those already packed, they had one hundred and sixty-five plew for their autumn's work—close to a thousand dollars' worth. And in those days and in that country such an amount was riches indeed!

While the skins were drying, John Barlow cut through the ice along the shore and brought mud to fill the spaces between the cabin logs. More poles were added to strengthen the roof against the weight of snow. And they fastened a thin-scraped square of deerskin over the window so that some light was let in though the cold was kept out.

With only his ax and knife for tools, Jeff's father also made a crude door, held together by wooden pegs and hinged with straps of thick buffalo hide. During this time Jeff was busy cutting wood. He stacked up three or four cords of it along the side of the cabin.

"All right," his father said with a grin one morning. "Time for us to go on a hunt."

It was frosty and still, with an overcast sky. So far no more snow had fallen, but there was a threat of it in the air now. They took their rifles, mounted their horses, and led one pack pony apiece. Five miles down the valley they sighted a small herd of buffalo on a distant slope. Leaving the horses tied in the edge of the woods, Jeff and his father went forward on foot.

"Not much wind," Barlow commented, holding up a wetted finger. "What there is is from the north, coming from them to us. Keep behind cover as long as you can. Then we'll crawl up within range."

The last hundred yards had to be made on their hands and knees, creeping through grass that was now brown and dry but offered some concealment. At last they came over a little rise and Jeff could see the buffalo feeding, so close it seemed almost a miracle the hunters hadn't been seen or heard.

"Take that cow on the right," Jeff's father whispered. "I'll pick another one. Wait till I nod my head."

They cocked the hammers of their rifles, took steady aim, and fired, almost together. Jeff saw two cows lurch forward and stumble to their knees. Bellowing, the rest of the herd broke into a gallop and was gone.

"You're getting to be an expert." Barlow chuckled. "Nice, clean heart shot, even with the light gun. You go back for the horses while I start on the skinning."

As he walked off down the slope, Jeff methodically reloaded his rifle. That was one of the rules he had learned in the months since he left St. Louis—never to wander around in the wilderness with an empty gun. Two or three minutes later the reason for it was brought home to him with some force.

He was still too far away to see the tethered horses, but he heard their frantic neighing. At a run he approached along the edge of the woods, afraid of what he might find. If it was Indians, he didn't know what he would do. Then he saw a gray shape sneaking close to the ponies. He recognized it as a timber wolf—and there were others among the trees. The horses huddled with their heads together, their heels lashing out at the attackers. Jeff was close enough now for a shot. He knelt for a better aim and let fly at the nearest wolf. It jumped four or five feet straight upward, gave a choked yelp of pain, and fell kicking to the ground. Jeff stayed where he was and reloaded.

To his surprise the other wolves—he could see three of them—still charged at the hocks of the horses, unfrightened by his shot. He ran closer, saw one of the animals clamp its jaws on the hind leg of a pack pony, and fired quickly. The wolf loosed its hold and turned to face him. Its big teeth were bared in a snarl. If he had hit it, the beast was still full of fight.

There was no time now to load the rifle. He grabbed it by the hot barrel and ran the few intervening yards, swinging the gun like a club. Then he saw that the wolf's hindquarters were crippled by the shot. It braced itself on powerful forelegs, opened its jaws wider, and lunged at him just as he struck downward. His blow missed, and the rifle flew out of his hands.

Jeff could have run back out of reach of the gray killer, but all he wanted now was to finish it. The heavy hunting knife was in his hand. He spun it in the quick gesture he had learned from Slim, and the blade drove true into the wolf's throat.

Panting, the boy recovered his rifle, made sure that it was undamaged, and put in powder and ball with shaky hands. The rest of the wolf pack had vanished into the woods. Jeff examined the hock of the pony that the second animal he had killed had been trying to hamstring. The wound was bleeding, but the tendon hadn't been cut.

He untied the four frightened horses, mounted his

own, and took the lead ropes. Leaving the two dead wolves, he rode back to where his father waited.

John Barlow looked up from his skinning. "What was the shooting about?" he asked. "See some more game?"

"Not just what you'd call game," Jeff answered with a grin. "It was wolves after the horses. I had to kill two of 'em before the others would run off."

"Lobos, eh? They get pretty bold this time o' year. Don't believe they can get into the corral, though. You'd better take that lame pony home and let Slim doctor his leg. Here, take along this first hide and the bundle o' meat."

The timber wolves had come back by the time Jeff reached the place where the horses had been tied. They were already starting to tear at their dead comrades but loped off at the sight of the boy. He stopped long enough to add the limp gray bodies to the load, while the horses shivered and trembled.

Back at camp, Slim went to work immediately on the pack pony's hock. With a balm of pine pitch and bear's grease he bandaged the wound and assured Jeff the animal would be as good as ever in a few days.

"Got a couple o' wolves, did ye?" he remarked. "Them hides'll make ye a warm winter jacket. Here, I'll show ye how to skin 'em right."

Soon Jeff's father came in with the meat and hide of the other buffalo, and that afternoon Pete and Slim took their turn at hunting. They were back by nightfall bringing still more buffalo meat. Slim had also shot a deer, which he turned over to Jeff. He knew the boy wanted to paint, and he explained that deerskin, properly tanned, would make a good surface to work on.

"That's what some o' the Injuns use," he said. "Bleach it with wood ashes an' it comes out nigh white."

They had built a high rack to hold the meat, and by

morning it was solidly frozen. Even in the shelter of the valley, temperatures stayed low all day now that winter had come, for the altitude must have been well over a mile above sea level. With game so plentiful, Jeff thought it would be an easy matter to store up enough meat to last till spring. But there was time for only one more hunt before the snow came.

It started in the night. There had been no stars in the sky when the boy looked out before going to bed. Some time later he woke to the wailing sound of wind around the cabin and the hissing of the driven flakes. The fire was out and he was cold. Stretching out his hand to pull another fold of blanket around him, he touched a little heap of snow that had drifted through the wall in spite of all their chinking. At last, rolled up like a cocoon, he got to sleep again.

In the morning the snow was still falling and drifting relentlessly. It kept it up for thirty hours. Finally, on the second morning, Jeff and his father were able to get the door open and shovel a path through drifts that were nearly as high as a man. They dug as far as the woodpile first, then on to the corral. Luckily a supply of sweet cottonwood bark had been stacked under the eaves of the cabin. When Jeff carried the first armful to the hungry horses, he found them gathered in a tight bunch in the middle of the pen. Their constant stamping and the warmth of their bodies had kept a little space clear, so that now they stood walled in by three-foot banks of snow. They whinnied gratefully at his approach and jostled each other to get at the fodder. In the last month the hair on their backs and legs had grown long and thick, and they looked almost as shaggy as buffalo.

Another path had to be dug to the grove of cottonwoods nearby, so that more bark could be peeled. After that chore, Jeff was at last ready to work on his own pet project.

Lying awake nights and thinking about it, he had figured out a way to make paintbrushes. He had saved a supply of stiffish hairs from a deerskin, and now he assembled a little tuft of them, all of even length. With gum from a pine tree, heated over the fire, he made a sort of glue to hold the hairs together at one end. Then he bound them firmly to a slim, foot-long stick, using deer sinew for the purpose. Before night he had finished three serviceable brushes and laid them up to dry.

Colors were going to be more difficult. There was plenty of vermilion powder in their trade goods, so he didn't need to worry about a bright red. He knew that pokeberry juice was sometimes used for blue and purple dye, but in winter he would never find any berries. What he needed most was a black that he could use for drawing outlines and filling in shadows. The end of a burnt stick was black enough, but even on a piece of white paper it dusted off too quickly to be of any value.

The second day after the storm he made his way over to Slim's cabin and asked the old trapper's advice. "You've been around Injuns a lot," he said. "How do they make black paint that'll stay on their faces?"

"Hmmm." Slim chuckled, rubbing his bristly chin. "You fixin' to go on the warpath, hoss?"

"Not right now," said the boy. "It's a poor time o' year for it. But I aim to draw some pictures while we're snowed in, and black paint would come in handy."

"Wal, now," the mountain man replied thoughtfully. "I kain't recollect ever seein' 'em make it, but I got a fair idee how it's done. Reckon they mix powdered charcoal with some sort o' grease—buffler or b'ar, most likely. No reason we shouldn't give her a try, anyhow."

They built a little pyramid of logs with a vent at the top and a stoke hole on the bottom at one side. Inside they stacked dry aspen sticks and built a fire under them.

"Ye want her to burn real slow—jest smolderin's best," said Slim. "Takes three days or more to git good charcoal. An' I reckon we'd oughter bank the sides with snow, all except the two holes."

Three days seemed like a long time to make something as simple as charcoal, but Jeff waited patiently. Daily he fed the fire and watched the slow curl of smoke coming from the top of the little log tepee. When the banked snow melted, he added more. Meanwhile, his father had insisted it was time he did some studying.

In their "possibles" they had brought along three books. One was a Bible, the second a thick, dog-eared volume of Shakespeare's plays, and the third a small dictionary. These served for all Jeff's school work except geography and arithmetic, subjects John Barlow had taught back in Illinois. He could draw amazingly accurate maps on the surface of the snow, and he knew all the capitals of states and countries by heart. When he gave his son arithmetic examples to work out, they usually dealt with everyday things like beaver, buffalo, horses, or gunpowder. One, for instance, was: "If one man uses three ounces of powder to kill nine buffalo, and his partner, with a lighter gun, uses only one ounce to bring down six buffalo in the same time, how much powder will they need for a total of ten buffalo, if they both hunt steadily?"

Jeff sweated over that one for close to an hour, but he finally came up with the right answer—two and two-thirds ounces.

When the charcoal was finished, Slim helped him take the little kiln apart. Inside they found nearly a bushel of sticks, nicely charred all the way through. Jeff stored most of them carefully in a corner of the cabin. Two or three he ground up at once, using a hollowed-out log and a round stone. When the charcoal was reduced to a smooth, black powder, he experimented with various mixtures of grease until at last he had a paint that satisfied him. It was almost pure black, and soft enough to use with his homemade brushes.

First he tried it on some of the paper he had brought in his pack. He outlined his picture lightly with a sharpened charcoal stick, getting the form and action right before he laid on the color. Working from memory, he drew a head and shoulders portrait of the old Crow chief, White Calf. It was exciting to try to catch the firm expression of the lean, high-cheekboned face, the narrowed eyes, shadowed by level brows, the great headdress of eagle feathers. And even though the only colors he had were vermilion and black, he was happy with the result.

When he had finished, he showed it to his father. Barlow looked at it, nodded, and said it was pretty good. Somewhat disappointed, Jeff carried the picture over to Slim's cabin.

"Know who this is s'posed to be?" he asked the old hunter.

Slim stared at the portrait, a delighted grin spreading over his face. "Wagh!" he cried. "Durned if you ain't drawed ol' White Calf! An' so nat'ral I kin 'most hear him speak. Boy, I'll give ye five prime beaver fer that picter!"

Jeff laughed. "This is just sort of a practice sketch," he said. "Don't waste your fur till you see how some o' the others turn out. Pa didn't seem to think so much of it, but I aim to make him admit I can draw 'fore I get through."

chapter 11

November ended and December came. There was no letup in the cold, though after that first big snow the sun shone steadily most of the time. The ponds were frozen over from bank to bank now, with ice thick enough to bear the weight of a man or even a horse.

Slim showed Jeff how to make a crude but serviceable pair of snowshoes. He used the hoops on which they had dried their beaver pelts, and strung them with a network of rawhide thongs, light and strong. On braces across the middle of each shoe he fastened straps to hold the toes of his moccasins.

It took several hours of practice before the boy could move with any speed on the awkward things, but he mastered the art at last. Then he was able to accompany the old mountain man on his hunts down the valley.

They saw occasional tracks of game in the snow, but the animals themselves were harder to find. Once Jeff almost stepped on some blacktail deer, bedded down in a thicket, and was only aware of their presence when they went bounding away. Most of the buffalo had left the valley for lower country and better grass. A few stragglers remained, and by careful stalking the hunters were able to shoot two that had yarded up in a box canyon. Luckily it was only a couple of miles from camp. Since they were unable to use the horses, they had to pack the meat and hides home on their backs.

The one kind of game that appeared to be plentiful was mountain sheep. Now that ice covered the high crags, the bighorn had come down from their summer pasture to paw away the snow in the bottoms and find grass. Fresh mutton made tasty eating, and Jeff was glad to get the hides, which proved to be at least as good as deerskin for painting.

All of the trappers hunted, but much of their time was spent working on new buckskin shirts, breeches, and moccasins. Slim gave Jeff his first instruction in how to prepare a deer's hide.

The skin first had to be soaked in ashes and water to loosen the hair. Then it was laid over what Slim called a graining block, shaped out of a short piece of log. The hair and the outer skin—the grain—was slowly scraped off with the blade of a knife. Next a mixture of fat and brains was rubbed deep into the hide—a long and tedious job. And finally the skin had to be pulled and stretched repeatedly until it became properly soft and pliable.

"To make real fine stuff," said Slim, "the Injun squaws put it in their mouths an' chaw on it fer days. That shore supples it up, but you ain't a squaw, so I reckon you don't want to bother."

Jeff was eager to have a whole outfit of buckskin, for the cloth garments he had worn all summer were now in rags. Under his father's guidance he cut the skins with his knife to a pattern taken from one of Barlow's old hunting shirts. Then, piercing the edges with an awl, he sewed the buckskin together with deer sinew.

From what he could see of himself in his father's little shaving mirror, it was a handsome piece of work. He had made a broad fringed collar to add to the dashing effect, and next he undertook to make a pair of fringed breeches. At the end of a week he was outfitted like a real mountain man.

Proudly he went over to the other cabin to show off his new finery. Pete was properly impressed, but Slim looked the boy over with a critical eye.

"Ye're quite a rooster, ain't ye?" he commented. "Too bad, though—thar's somethin' missin'. Here—try this on fer size."

As he spoke, he tossed a furry object in Jeff's direction. When he caught it, he was astonished to find a coonskin cap in his hand. It was fresh winter fur, and the bushy, ringed tail was attached.

"Shot this feller last week," the old trapper said with a chuckle. "Figgered ye might need somethin' to keep yer haid warm."

The cap was a good fit. Wearing it, along with the buckskins, and carrying the Kentucky rifle, Jeff felt like old Dan'l Boone himself.

A supply of moccasins, cut from buffalo and elk hide, still had to be made, but once that task was out of the way their wardrobes were complete. Jeff went back to his painting.

He used the last of his paper to make small color sketches that would catch the action he wanted to put into larger pictures. Several good-sized pieces of deerskin, carefully cured and bleached, were ready now. He stretched one tight over a rectangular frame he had made and started outlining a hunting scene in charcoal. It showed young Running Wolf on his piebald horse in hot pursuit of a buffalo bull. The chief's son was leaning forward, the bowstring pulled back clear to his ear and the heavy hunting arrow aimed straight at the bull's heart.

As he drew, the boy's own muscles tensed and he

breathed hard, feeling again the wild excitement of the chase. He could even put himself in the pony's place—neck outstretched and nostrils flaring, hoofs pounding over the ground. The result was a picture packed with action. He stood back from it and stared, surprised at its vivid realism. His father came and looked silently over his shoulder. At last he nodded.

"I don't know how you do it, son," he said, "but you've got the gift—no question about it. The Indian and the pony couldn't be better. They're going all out for the kill. Only criticism I could make is that the buffalo's legs might be a shade too long. Even a big bull doesn't stand as tall as a horse, you know."

"Gee, Pa, you're right," said Jeff. "But I can fix that easy. I'm mighty glad you think the rest of it's good."

That night he felt spent—almost as tired as if he had been galloping after buffalo all day. But there was a wonderful sense of accomplishment, too. He had discovered once more the joy of artistic creation.

In the weeks that followed he worked at his painting steadily. Nearly all the deer and sheepskin was used up now, and before the end of December he had to put on his snowshoes and go after more hides.

The first snow had crusted over. Since then another foot or more had fallen, and it still lay deep and feathery, leveling the floor of the valley with a soft white blanket. Jeff tramped down the creek bank for nearly three miles without a glimpse of any deer or even deer tracks. With some difficulty he worked his way westward into the woods, hoping to come upon a hidden "yard" where the blacktails might be wintering. Still his search was fruitless. Discouraged, he was about ready to start back when he caught sight of something moving up on the ledges behind the trees.

Stepping very softly and slowly, he changed position till

he had a better view. There were three bighorn sheep up there on the higher rocks where wind had swept off most of the snow. They were nearly three hundred yards away, but he could see them plainly—two ewes and a monster ram.

For a moment all Jeff could do was stand there, his unbelieving eyes on the great male sheep. Its horns were larger than anything he had imagined—each as big as a man's thigh where it grew out of the massive head. They swept outward, curling magnificently in more than a full circle. It was no wonder, Jeff thought, that the animal had such a thick and powerful neck. A lot of muscle would be needed to hold those hundred-pound horns proudly aloft.

The range was too great for accurate shooting, yet the boy hesitated to move any nearer. If he stepped out beyond the fringe of the woods, he was sure the sheep would see him. In loading his rifle, he had put in a little more powder than usual, and he thought it was possible the heavy charge might carry that far. Steadying the long barrel across a limb, he took a careful sight on the ram, aiming behind the shoulder. But just as he was ready to squeeze the trigger, one of the females moved slowly across till she blocked his shot.

He waited and held his breath, but there she stayed. Then he saw the ram's head lifted, sniffing the breeze. If some human scent had reached that keen nose, the sheep would all be gone in a flash. It was now or never, and he fired at the ewe's side, holding a little high because of the distance.

The report echoed from the rocks. He saw the female rear upward, then topple from the ledge. And the ram and his other consort went bounding away out of sight around a corner of the cliff.

Jeff knew he had made a good shot, and though he had hoped to get the ram, he felt oddly elated now that the great beast was safe. Nobody would ever believe him when he described those tremendous horns, but deep inside him he was glad. He scrambled up to the dead sheep and went about taking the hide and the meat. As he worked, another comforting thought came to him. If he had killed the ram, he could never in the world have carried the head back to camp.

He skinned the sheep with care, thinking of the use he could make of her hide. One picture he meant to paint was her giant mate, standing guard over his ewes. The scene was sharply imprinted in his memory, and those who saw the painting could believe it or not, as they liked. He, at least, would know it was true.

As soon as he got back to camp, he started working on the skin. It would take perhaps a week to cure it properly, and he didn't want to waste any time.

Christmas came before the boy had even thought about it. He looked up from his work on the hide one afternoon and saw his father bringing a little fir tree from the woods.

"We won't have any decorations for it," said John Barlow, "but at least it'll be a reminder that this is Christmas Eve."

He set the tree up in a corner of the cabin, and that night by the light of the fire, he read Jeff the account of Jesus' birth from the tattered old Bible. They went to sleep with the sense of peace and good will still upon them.

In the morning they woke to hear Slim's "Merry Christmas!" outside the cabin. And close behind him was Pete, calling a "Joyeux Noël!"

"Hey," said Slim, "soon as ye've et, come on down to our place an' see what Pete's been up to." The Frenchman only grinned and kicked at the snow with the toe of his moccasin.

When they reached the lower cabin, Jeff and his father saw an arrangement of fir boughs beside the door. Coming nearer, they discovered it was a little *crèche,* with a manger and figures roughly carved out of wood. There was Mary, robed in red trade calico, holding the little Jesus in her stiff arms. Joseph stood near them, and a wooden cow looked on. In front of the *crèche* a small candle burned.

"Ain't that purty?" asked Slim. "He's been workin' nights fer nigh a month to make it."

"It's beautiful, Pete," said John Barlow quietly. "I didn't know you had it in you."

Jeff felt a new warmth for the stocky Frenchman. He knew him as a hard, stubborn worker. Now he saw that

Pete had a gentler side. Crude as the carvings were, they had been done with love and tenderness.

The only presents given that Christmas Day were some of Jeff's sketches, which he had saved for the purpose. He gave Slim the paper portrait sketch of White Calf, and his father a preliminary drawing of the two fighting elk. One other, a picture of a beaver gnawing at a tree, he presented to Pete LeBlanc.

That evening Slim thawed out some choice pieces of buffalo hump, and they all ate together, making a feast of it.

"Doggone!" said Slim. "Only thing missin' is a good slug o' whisky. You shore you ain't got a leetle red-eye cached in them trade goods, Jawn?"

Jeff's father laughed. "You know me better than that," he told the old trapper. "I never used the stuff myself, and I don't believe in getting an Indian drunk to get the best of him in a trade. I know they do it at most o' the posts, but it never set well with me."

Slim shook his head sadly. "Any other feller tol' me that," he said, "I'd shore take him fer a hymn-singin' preacher. It's a miracle you turned out to be sech a good mountain man, Jawn, with no bad habits to season ye."

It snowed again that night and a fierce wind shook the cabin. Snug beneath his buffalo robes, Jeff pitied the horses, huddled out there in their stockade. It would be rough on the other animals, too, he thought. The deer and elk in their trampled yards, and the few buffalo left at the lower end of the valley—how did they manage to live through a blizzard? Only the bears, denned up for the winter, and the beaver, housed in their lodges, could be comfortable in such weather.

By midday the snow had stopped falling, but the wind still blew, piling up fresh drifts. Jeff and his father spent most of the brief afternoon digging out their paths. They were able to reach the corral before nightfall, and carried armfuls of cottonwood bark to the half-frozen horses. Only eight ponies responded to the lure of fodder. Two had died in the blizzard, and their bodies lay under the drifted snow. Little by little the weather was taking its toll of their pack animals.

"It's what you've got to expect when you winter in the high country," Jeff's father told him. "It's rough to lose 'em, and it'll be rough on us, too, when we start packing out in the spring. Just be thankful your saddle pony's still standing up to it."

Jeff found it difficult to take this attitude. He wasn't yet hardened to the stern philosophy of the mountain men. For them, horses were like powder and lead. They were expendable.

When the sun came out the next day, the boy recovered some of his spirits. The valley lay glistening white under its fresh blanket. A few hardy birds, chickadees and Canada jays, chirped and fluttered in the pine trees.

Jeff put on his snowshoes and went for a hunt with Slim. They tramped a long way down the valley before they saw any tracks, but at last the old mountain man pointed to a sort of trough in the snow, leading toward a clump of woods.

"Wolves," he said. "Hard goin' fer 'em, belly deep like that. Must ha' smelled game, though. What say we foller 'em, hoss?"

The floundering trail split into two at the edge of the pine thicket. The wolves had separated to scout the area from two directions.

"Quiet now," the old man whispered. "Reckon thar's a deer yard somewheres in the middle."

They bent low to creep under the snow-laden pine boughs and went silently forward into the thicket. After a dozen yards Slim held up a warning hand. Looking over his companion's shoulder, Jeff could see the antlers of a blacktail buck above the snow. The animal's huge ears twitched nervously as it tested the air for hostile sounds.

At that moment there was a flurry in the drifts over to the left. Jeff caught a flashing glimpse of a grayish-white body as a big timber wolf sprang toward the deer. Slim's rifle barked, and the gray beast fell back with a gasping yelp.

"Go ahead," said the mountain man calmly as he reloaded. "Git yerself a deer. Me—I jest kain't stand them lobo wolves."

By this time the yarded blacktails were in a frenzy of terror. One of the does cleared the high bank of snow with a tremendous bound, only to sink downward, buried deep in a drift. Before she could free herself, Jeff sent a bullet into her heart.

The others were still huddled in their yard, but the boy paid no attention to them. As he cut the dead deer's throat, he had a bitter feeling that he was no better than the wolf. Both of them killed for meat.

chapter 12

Sometimes it seemed as if the harsh winter months would never end. Yet Jeff was far happier than he might have been if he had had no occupation but hunting and making buckskin clothes. His father insisted on two or three hours of schoolwork every day. Reading—usually from Shakespeare or the Bible—writing, spelling, geography, and arithmetic took up the time. In addition, he had firewood to cut and fodder to carry. But when these tasks were done, he could bury himself in his painting.

The pile of stretched skins grew slowly as he experimented with line and color. His brushwork improved, and he learned new techniques that made his pictures more lifelike in spite of their being limited to black and red. Jeff's greatest gifts were a vivid memory for form and action and the ability to re-create them with the tools he held in his fingers.

The picture of the great ram took longer than any of the others, but he felt it was the best he had done. There was little chance for color in it—just the black of the crag, the white snow, and the pale gray of the bighorns' bodies. Yet he caught the proud lift of the ram's head and those incredible horns and knew he had them right.

His father looked at the finished painting and gave a nod of approval. "I've seen 'em myself, looking just like that," he said. "Handsome animals—those cimarron sheep. Didn't exaggerate the horns just a mite, did you?"

"No, Pa, I didn't," Jeff replied soberly. "They were that big, honest, but I wouldn't expect any of you to believe it."

John Barlow smiled. "I believe it," he said. "You see, I spotted that ram myself, a week or so ago."

That was as close as Jeff's father ever came to praising his work, but the boy knew he was pleased and impressed. He could almost see the way Barlow's mind was working. An educated man, he had never scoffed at the idea of his son's turning into an artist. True, he had brought him west to teach him self-reliance, but not necessarily to make him a mountain man. Jeff had seen his eyes light up at some of the sketches. If he had been sparing in his spoken praise, it was probably because he was afraid of giving his son inflated ideas.

None of the four in their party was sick a day that winter. Not even a cold came to bother them. John Barlow said it was the clear mountain air that kept them healthy. Slim attributed it to the fact that they ate nothing but fresh or frozen meat.

"City folks, livin' on bread an' vegetables an' sweet stuff, are sickly half the time," the old man snorted. "Only time this coon ever gits to feelin' porely is in town, eatin' town vittles. An'," he added, catching sight of Barlow's grin, "I ain't referrin' to town liquor, neither!"

January passed and February. Early in March, as the sun rose higher over the mountains each day, they had their first thaw. It came with a soft breeze from the south—what Slim called a "chinook" wind. All night Jeff could hear the melting snow running off the eaves and down the hills in rivulets of water that flooded the ice-covered ponds.

When morning came, the chickadees and jays flew everywhere, noisy with the promise of spring.

Actually, as John Barlow prophesied, this was just a thaw, soon to be followed by more snow and more freezing nights. But the hard clutch of winter was breaking. Before another month passed, the ice went out of the stream and the beaver were at work again. It was time for the spring trapping.

The fur was still prime, but the water was so cold that Jeff had to run up and down on the bank to warm his legs after each trap was set. He was amazed at the daily catches. It seemed as if the beaver, after their period of lethargy, had forgotten all fear of traps and fell an easy prey to the lure of castrum. In three busy weeks the mountain men caught enough fur to fill five more packs.

By the end of that time Slim was beginning to get restless. "The rendezvous'll be held pretty quick," he told Jeff's father. "Bet thar's some o' the comp'ny men over on the Green right now. If'n we aim to git thar 'fore the tradin's over, we'd better be makin' plans to break camp."

John Barlow grinned. "Beginning to get a thirst, aren't you, Slim? Still, I reckon you may be right. We've got all the fur now that the pack horses can carry. What's our best route to reach the South Pass?"

"Wal," said Slim, "this child's been givin' it thought. Thar's two ways. One—we'd hev to cross them dry plains, same way we come, an' then head back up the Sweetwater. T'other way'd be to climb the west wall o' the valley an' cut acrost through the Wind River Mountains. Terrible rough goin', prob'ly, but if we make it, we'd come out jest a skip an' a jump from the pass."

Barlow nodded thoughtfully. "I'd vote for the first way," he said, "for a couple of reasons. We could cache part of our fur along the Sweetwater, where it can be picked up by the company men on their way downriver. That way we

wouldn't have to pack it all the way across to the Green—just enough to do what trading we want to at the rendezvous. What's more, we'd be traveling a trail we know. That 'skip an' a jump' o' yours might turn out to be a hundred miles, and no telling how many mountains to climb."

Slim sniffed with a touch of hurt pride. However, he had to admit his estimate of the distance westward was a pure guess. And Pete LeBlanc, being less adventurous, favored Barlow's plan. It was finally decided that they would pick up the traps, bale the dried skins, and be ready to start in three days.

The grass was green now in the bottoms, and the horses were beginning to put on some of the flesh they had lost during the winter. They would be in shape for the long, dry march to the Sweetwater.

It was the twentieth day of April when their preparations were finished. Each of the four pack ponies was loaded with three hundred pounds of skins, along with traps, blankets, and utensils. Another bale of fur was strapped on behind each rider's saddle. And in addition to their rifles, they carried full canteens and enough jerked meat for the journey. Jeff had made a compact bundle of his deerskin paintings.

The morning was bright and clear. John Barlow looked back over the little line of men and horses and waved his arm in a gesture that started them toward the head of the valley. The ponies, fresh and well rested, tackled the slope eagerly. Within an hour they were over the rim and headed southward.

After a last, lingering look at the beauty of the valley below, Jeff faced the dry plateau without dread. He was a toughened mountain man now and felt ready for any kind of hardship. Actually the trip seemed easier this time. The heat was less intense, and there were even a few half-dried water holes left from the melting snow. It was a comfort, too, to see patches of tiny flowers blooming in the arid waste.

They made an estimated thirty miles before darkness fell and camped close to a "sink" that held a few inches of brackish water. Slim tasted it and made a face but assured them it could be drunk with no ill effects. They brewed tea, chewed on pieces of jerky, and went to sleep with their saddles for pillows. At daybreak they were off once more.

The sun was well down toward the western mountains next day when the cavalcade reached the bluffs above the Sweetwater. Smelling water and grass, the ponies were hard to hold. Pete's pack horse broke away and went headlong down the cliff, sliding, stumbling, and finally rolling. The thongs that held the pack burst. It took the Frenchman the best part of an hour to collect the scattered pelts and carry them down to the riverbank, where the others were making camp.

"Sacré nom!" grumbled LeBlanc. "Dat hoss, she need a fas' keeck in de haid, for sho'!"

He went over to the pony, now munching grass, none the worse for the tumble. But instead of dealing out punishment, he felt the bruised legs and patted the beast on the rump.

"Tenderhearted cuss," said Slim with a chuckle. "But 'twa'n't rightly the pony's fault. He didn't have the lead rope tied proper."

Around the fire that night they made further plans. The bulk of the fur had to be safely buried where nobody else would find it. Jeff's father had already picked a spot while he was foraging for firewood.

"It's in a patch o' brush," he said, "back yonder at the foot o' the cliff. Come morning the rest of us'll dig the hole while you go out and get us some meat, Slim."

"Suits me," said the older man with a laugh. "Never was real partial to diggin', nohow."

The cache his father planned was more than just a hole in the ground, Jeff discovered. They dug steadily for two hours till it was three or four feet across and a good six feet deep. Then a shaft, or tunnel, was started from the bottom of the pit, running back toward the cliff. It sloped upward, so that the stored furs would stay dry in any kind of weather. Not until midafternoon was it finished to Barlow's satisfaction. By that time Wind River Slim had returned.

He had shot a blacktail buck and had the meat and hide across his saddle. "Game ain't as plenty as I'd figgered," he announced. "No sign o' buffler, an' this feller was all by his lonesome. Somebody must ha' been through lately an' skeert 'em off."

"Trappers, maybe," suggested Jeff's father, "heading up to the pass for the rendezvous. Did you see any horse tracks?"

Slim shook his head. "No, but it don't signify," he said. "Looks like thar'd been rain a couple o' days back, so tracks would ha' been washed out."

They carried twelve packs of beaver up to the prepared hideaway and stacked them safely in the shaft before supper. Slim would have kept more of his catch to take west with him, but Barlow persuaded him that one pack was enough to buy all the whisky he could possibly drink.

"You'll be glad to have credit when you get down to St. Louis," he argued. "On forty or fifty plew you'll be able to live high till you start back to the mountains."

They worked till dark, covering the cache with brush and smoothing away all traces of their digging. Then, back at the campfire, they dined royally on fresh venison and liver. It was a fine, clear night. The horses were gathered contentedly, close to the riverbank, and they left them there unpicketed. With so much good grass handy it was unlikely any of them would stray.

The water was high with spring freshets, and as Jeff lay in his blanket, he could hear the lapping of the river among the stones on the shore. Otherwise the night was quiet. No wolves or coyotes disturbed the silence with their howling. Peacefully the boy went to sleep, thinking of new adventures on the morrow when they would take the trail to the Green River rendezvous.

In the gray half-light before dawn he woke to a sound of sudden commotion. A pounding of hoofs came from the meadow by the riverbank. His father stumbled past him, rifle in hand, and he could hear Slim growling curses. As soon as he gathered his wits, he grabbed for his gun and scrambled up. And at that moment there came a triumphant whoop from a little distance downstream.

Jeff knew what had happened, even before he joined his father. With a sick feeling he realized that Indians had run off the horse herd. Ahead, in the little meadow where the ponies had been bedded, the only living thing was Wind River Slim. He stood there shaking his fist to the eastward and swearing with such force and fluency as Jeff had never heard before.

With Pete's arrival they all stood there looking glumly down the river. At last Slim ran out of epithets. He sat down and stabbed his knife viciously into the sand.

"I'll git them stinkin' red skunks," he panted, "if'n it's the last thing I do, so help me! Should ha' knowed 'twas too quiet 'round here last night."

"Well," said John Barlow more calmly, "at least we can have breakfast. Start a fire, Jeff, and we'll talk over what to do while we eat."

Now that Slim's first rage was past, he got up and started searching the ground along the bank above their camp. By the time the food was ready he was back.

"Who were they?" asked Barlow. "And how many?"

"Snakes or Cheyennes, I reckon," said the old hunter. "Headed east, so my guess is they're Cheyennes. I count eight hosses—mebbe one or two more, but not over ten of 'em in all."

"War party, you think?"

"More likely a bunch o' young bucks tryin' to make *coup*. They're out o' their country. Prob'ly come up this way lookin' fer buffler or hosses. Don't reckon they was after ha'r, but they'd be glad to take it if'n they found it."

Jeff's father nodded thoughtfully. "I'd say we've got two choices, now that we're stranded here afoot," he said. "One is just to wait a month or so, till Sublette or Fitzpatrick or some o' the other Fur Company men come down the river after the rendezvous. The other would be to kill two or three buffalo, make ourselves bullboats, and try to get our own fur down to St. Louis."

"Humph!" Slim snorted. "Ever try to steer a bullboat in white water? This coon reckons thar's a third thing we could do."

Barlow smiled a little and nodded. "I thought so," he said. "All right, old-timer, let's hear it."

"I seen it done before," Slim told them apologetically, "or I wouldn't be suggestin' it now. I was with Fitzpatrick an' some o' the boys the fust year we crossed the South Pass an' found the Green. Trappin' was good an' we was takin' fur hand over fist. But we got careless about keepin' a hoss guard. One mornin' jest before light, like this mornin', a party o' Snakes—Shoshones—run off our whole herd an' left us madder'n a flock o' wet hens.

"Thar wa'n't but a dozen of us, an' some was hardly more'n tenderfeet. But that didn't bother Fitz. He put us to work cachin' our beaver an' traps. Then each man took his rifle an' a leetle food an' off we went, trailin' the Injuns afoot. They'd rid hard fer two days, but after that we found their campin' places closer together. In about a week our moccasins was wore out, but we'd come in sight o' their village—a big 'un—fifty or sixty lodges. That night we scouted the hoss herd an' found it was feedin' downwind from the village, close to some woods. So we crawled 'round 'em, each man grabbed a hoss, an' we stampeded the hull herd right through the lodges. Got clean away before an arrer could hit us. We didn't lack fer mounts or pack ponies after that. Had 'em by the hundred!"

There was a pause while Barlow and LeBlanc thought it over. Pete was a heavy man, and he sighed at the thought of the long, forced marches that would be necessary. But when Jeff's father favored the plan, he reluctantly agreed.

Jeff was still in a daze. The loss of his buckskin—the

first horse he had ever really owned—had been a blow he found hard to bear. But the decision to go after the Indians cheered him up. Here was a real adventure—one he hadn't counted on!

chapter 13

The sun was only half an hour high when they started. All their heavier belongings, including saddles and spare clothing, had been carefully cached. They carried nothing but absolute essentials and went in single file, Slim leading the way. His keen old eyes were constantly on the tracks left by the marauders. He moved at a slouching, bent-kneed walk that covered ground fast, and Jeff, next in line, was hard put to keep up with him.

The Indians had driven the ponies at a run for the first few miles, then settled to a slower gait. They still followed the riverbank.

"Reckon they ain't very skeert of us," said Slim. "They prob'ly scouted our camp last night—seen thar wa'n't but three men an' a boy. That's why they don't 'pear to be in much of a hurry. Right along here you kin see the hosses was walkin'."

The sun blazed down hot in the valley, but Slim kept up his steady, swinging pace. About noon they came to a spot where the band had halted to let the ponies drink. The old hunter knelt and examined the tracks in the mud.

"Not more'n two hours old," he announced. "That close,

we'd best go keerful. They might have a scout out, guardin' their rear."

From that point on, the four white men kept in the cover of the cottonwoods, with only an occasional sortie by Slim to make sure the fresh trail was still there. Poor Pete was sweating and panting, and Jeff's feet were getting heavier, mile by mile. It must have been five o'clock in the afternoon when the old mountain man held up a hand and signaled them to stop. The others drew around him. He pointed to the prints of many hoofs heading northeastward, away from the river.

"They turned off here, not more'n an hour ago," he whispered. "Could be thar's a bigger party back in the hills they're aimin' to jine. That'd mean we're plumb out o' luck. But mebbe they're jest headin' fer a place to camp. Stay here an' git some rest whilst I go take a leetle look. One thing ye might do is cut some rawhide thongs off this skin I brung along. If'n we do make a try fer the hosses, we'll need 'em."

Without a sound he vanished into the woods. Jeff and his father got out their hunting knives and sliced long, thin strips off the edge of the hide.

"We can use these a couple o' ways," John Barlow told Jeff in answer to a question. "One is to tie our rifles on our backs—leave both hands free so we can grab a pony and get aboard him. The other might be to throw a loop around a horse's jaw for a rein like the Indians use."

Slim was gone a long time. It was almost dark when he came back to join them.

"Lost their trail," the old hunter grumbled. "Thar's a leetle creek up a ways an' they waded their hosses, prob'ly upstream. Oughta be easy to pick it up again in daylight, but right now I reckon we'd do better to rest an' make an early start."

They ate some jerked meat and used the water in their canteens. As a precaution, they took turns standing guard that night. Jeff had the first watch and was able to get to sleep by eleven o'clock. Before five in the morning his father roused him out.

"Be light enough to see tracks soon," he said. "We've got to be on our way."

Slim led them to the place where the Indians' ponies had entered the stream, and they filled their canteens there. "Two of us kin go up each side," said the veteran mountain man. "Fust sign o' tracks comin' out o' the water, we'll signal. But don't holler. Jest give a jaybird whistle."

Jeff and his father took the near bank while Pete and Slim crossed over. They moved as quietly as they could, avoiding dead sticks as they climbed over the rocks and fallen trees. Half an hour passed and still there was no sign of hoofprints. At last they came to a place where the water tumbled over a ten-foot fall.

Slim appeared on the farther bank and shook his head disgustedly. "Outfoxed us," he said. "They doubled back an' went downstream, 'stead of up. If'n they'd come this far, they'd ha' had to leave the creek."

It was disheartening to turn and retrace their steps. It meant the Indians had lengthened their lead, perhaps by half a day.

"Looks as if they'd guessed we were following," Barlow told his son. "That'll make it harder to catch 'em off guard."

A mile below the place where they had first reached the stream, they heard the low, chuckling whistle of a Canada jay. Slim stuck his head out of the brush on the opposite bank and beckoned to them to cross. The water was only two or three feet deep, and in a moment they were on dry land again, following a well-marked trail eastward. Slim went almost at a lope now, trying to recover lost ground.

After two or three miles they came to a trampled place among some trees where the horses had been picketed. Nearby there were signs that the Indians had built a small fire.

"They slep' here," said Slim, bending over the ground near the fire. "Not long, I reckon, but they was here part o' the night."

He pointed to one clear moccasin track. "I told ye they was Cheyennes, an' this proves it. The squaws in every tribe make their moccasins a leetle different. See the way the outer sole is sewed on? If'n they didn't git started till daylight, we ain't but about three or four hours behind."

Doggedly they picked up the trail again, hurrying along behind the old hunter. Within a few minutes Jeff realized they were coming back to the Sweetwater. To him it seemed like a good omen. It looked as if the Indians must have decided their maneuver had got rid of any pursuit. And a moment later his idea was borne out.

"They've quit pushin'," said Slim with satisfaction. "See there? They're lettin' the hosses walk. All we got to do now is tag along steady, but I reckon we'd better stick to cover."

The four trappers went on with no stops for rest. They munched strips of dried venison and drank a little water, but kept moving. Jeff forgot all about being tired. He knew they were holding their own with the Cheyennes. When he found breath enough, he asked Slim what he had meant about the Indians trying to "make *coup*."

"Wal," said the old man, "a young buck ain't reelly a man till he kin prove he's brave an' smart. Ever' time he steals a hoss, or kills a buffler, or takes a scalp, he counts *coup*. He keeps a *coup* stick with a sort o' record o' what he's done. Mebbe it's got a wolf scalp on it, an' a bunch o' ha'r pulled out of a pony's tail. Stealin' hosses ain't rightly dishonest, the way an Injun thinks. It's sort of a game.

'Course, the hoss has to be took from an enemy tribe or a white man to give him any credit.

"I wouldn't be surprised," he went on, "if this bunch is all youngsters, yore age or less. Prob'ly out on their first long hunt beyond their own country."

They kept going till well after sunset. Then, in the gathering dusk, John Barlow took over the scouting duty. He moved off through the trees, silent-footed as a shadow. This was no time to build a cook fire. Slim, Pete, and Jeff sat down to rest and chewed hungrily on the last of their jerked meat. Then, one by one, they crept down to the riverbank, a few yards away, to slake their thirst.

Jeff's father was back much sooner than the boy expected. He appeared suddenly out of the dark, one hand held up in a warning for silence. Then he knelt close to them and whispered his report. "They've made camp," he said, "only about half a mile from here. It's up from the river in a little box canyon. The horses are loose, back toward the rocks at the upper end, and they've got their fires lit down near the entrance. I could hear 'em talking and laughing. Counted eight men, all young bucks, as you said, Slim. Far as I could tell they don't have any scouts out."

"How 'bout them rocks above the canyon?" Slim asked. "Kin we git in thar behind 'em, you reckon?"

"I think so. And the wind's right—blowing up from the south."

"Good," said Slim. "Better wait two-three hours till they're sound asleep."

Tired as Jeff was, he found it difficult to take a nap. For what seemed an interminable time he lay there twisting and turning, his mind on the action ahead. Then without knowing it he dropped off. It was his father who woke him, shaking his shoulder.

"Time to go," he whispered. "And remember—we've got to keep mighty quiet to pull this off."

In single file they followed John Barlow's lead through the darkness. He didn't hurry them. It was rough going, and they had to pick their way carefully. Soon they were climbing, helping each other up the steep rocks. Then Jeff's father made a turn to the right. He moved along a ledge that seemed to run level for some distance.

Looking over the tops of the trees below, Jeff could see the dark outlines of the little canyon. There was no sign of the horse herd from that position, but two or three hundred yards away the embers of dying fires glowed faintly.

John Barlow gathered the others close to him and pointed down through the woods. "The horses are right there," he breathed, "not more than fifty yards off. Slim, you take over. Tell us what to do."

The old mountain man wet a finger and held it up. "Wind's still blowin' from them to us," he whispered. "We'll jest crawl down through the woods, good an' quiet. Soon as we're in the open, go on yer bellies. Git as clost as ye kin, then run fer the nearest hoss. Grab his mane an' git on his back. Then foller me an' do as I do."

Slim had slung his rifle behind his shoulders with the rawhide thong, and now the others followed his example. Then they were moving slowly down the rocks and in among the trees. In the thick darkness it was difficult to make no noise, but luck seemed to be with them. They were almost through when Pete stepped on a dry stick. The crackle was hardly audible. Yet Jeff heard the startled snort of a horse, so near it made him hold his breath.

For three or four seconds they all lay motionless. Then Slim was going on again, wriggling along the ground like a snake. The moment they reached the end of the woods they could see the big dark shapes of the horses, some of them only a dozen yards away.

"Now!" whispered Slim. He rose to a crouching position

and waited till his companions had done the same. Then he was off with a bound.

Jeff found himself racing at top speed toward a pony that seemed paler in color than the rest. He was still a stride away when the herd took alarm, but he lunged forward desperately and locked his fingers in the animal's mane. His momentum carried him halfway up the horse's side, and he scrambled aboard, clinging tight with his knees.

Off to his left there was an ear-splitting whoop, as old Slim lashed his mount straight into the jostling, frightened ponies. There were nearly twenty of them. Now the other white men began to yell, and in another second the whole bunch stampeded down the canyon.

In the middle of the wild rush Jeff hung on, bent low over his pony's neck. The herd went thundering through the camp at a dead run. Almost under his horse's hoofs the boy saw a sleep-dazed Indian roll sidewise, still struggling to get out of his blanket. Then, before a single arrow could be discharged or a tomahawk thrown, they were out of the canyon.

John Barlow and Slim had ridden out to the left in time to turn the stampede at the riverbank and head the galloping horses westward. Now they brought up the rear while Jeff and Pete rode as flankers, keeping the herd on the trail. After a brief struggle, Jeff had succeeded in getting the loop of a rawhide thong around the lower jaw of his mount and was able to control him. With some delight he realized that he was riding his own buckskin!

The wild run continued for nearly an hour before some of the horses were winded. Their progress slowed to a trot then, but still they moved faster than the Cheyennes could follow afoot. A little before daylight Slim suggested that they give the tired ponies a short rest and a chance to drink.

"We've come better'n a dozen miles," he said. "An' after the way we rid over 'em, them bucks ain't likely to be doin'

much chasin'. What we need now is to keep movin' steady till we git to our supplies. This coon, fer one, could shore do with some eatin'."

Before midday, hot, dusty, and panting with fatigue, the cavalcade reached the place where the fur was cached. In ten hours they had covered as much distance as they had traveled in the previous two days on foot.

The ponies, both their own and the Indians', were watered, hobbled, and let out to graze. Then Jeff started a cooking fire, and they enjoyed their first real meal in what seemed like a long time.

Wind River Slim lay back contentedly and filled his pipe. "Wal, boys," he said with a chuckle, "we pulled it off. Nary a shot fired an' we come back with twicet as many hosses as what we started with. Ol' Fitz hisself'd be jealous o' the way we managed it. Maybe he'll be at the rendezvous, an' this child'll shore tell him."

chapter 14

They rested for two hours, and Jeff took a nap in the shade of a cottonwood tree. When he woke, it was to the sound of loud, cheerful voices. He sat up, stared, and rubbed his eyes. Down by the riverbank he was amazed to see a dozen buckskin-clad mountain men! After all the months in which his world had been made up of only three others besides himself, the little group looked like a multitude.

Hastily he picked up his rifle and went to join them. Slim was in his element. All these trappers were old friends of his, and he moved from one to another, slapping them on the back, yelling their names, cursing joyfully, and letting out savage war whoops.

His father called to Jeff and introduced him to several of the new arrivals. He had heard some of the names before and knew they were famous from the Missouri to the Columbia. Shyly he shook hands with young Jim Bridger, the great Fitzpatrick, and the leader of the party, Bill Sublette himself. Some of the men with them, he learned, were free trappers, others working for General Ashley's Rocky Mountain Fur Company. They had their winter's beaver loaded on pack horses and were on their way to the Green River rendezvous.

"See any Injuns down the river a piece?" Slim asked Fitzpatrick with a grin. "If'n ye did, I bet they was afoot."

"Cain't say we ketched sight of any," Fitz replied. "What's yore story?"

With considerable relish, Slim described the capture and recovery of their ponies. " 'Twa'n't reelly nothin'," he said in conclusion. "Any mountain man that remembered that raid the Snakes made our fust year on the Siskeedee would ha' knowed how to bring it off."

Fitzpatrick's eyes twinkled. "We did figger ye must ha' brung along a power o' hosses, when we rid up," he said. "Glad to hear ye ain't fergot all I taught ye."

Slim pretended to be indignant. "Why, blast yore hide!" he snorted. "This hoss was ketchin' beaver on the Big Horn when you was no more'n a shirttail young'un!"

One of the Ashley men had shot an elk that morning, and there was enough fresh meat for all. More to the point, as far as Slim and Pete were concerned, the newcomers had brought along a small, flat pack-keg of trade whisky. By the time darkness fell enough liquor had been passed around to set the camp in an uproar. Songs were sung and old jokes told and there were even a few arguments, settled harmlessly by wrestling matches in the sand of the riverbank.

"Son," said John Barlow as the evening wore on, "as long as they're having their fun, I guess it's up to us to stand watch. You take it till midnight and then call me. These boys'll be dead to the world by that time."

Sure enough, the party began to grow quieter after a time. One man after another stumbled to his blankets or began snoring right where he happened to lie. Finally only Slim, Fitz, and Bill Sublette were left awake. Jeff, sitting a little way off, listened to their talk and was fascinated. They spoke of such legendary mountain men as Jed Smith, half preacher, half fighter, who read his Bible every day, wherever he happened to be. And they spoke of General Ashley, who had struggled for years and finally established the Rocky Mountain Fur Company. It was on a solid footing now, in spite of hardship and disaster and rough competition from the Missouri Company and the Hudson's Bay Company.

"Talked to the Gin'ral 'fore we left," said Sublette. "He's still tryin' to protect the lone trappers, like you, Slim, an' Barlow, an' the rest. Makin' it pay, too. The other outfits, like the Americans on the upper Missouri an' the British on the Columbia, still depend on their hired trappers an' Injuns for all their fur. We git a good half of ourn from folks like you."

Slim nodded, drained his tin cup, and stretched his long arms. "Time to git to bed." He yawned. "I told ye young Barlow's a mountain man. Thar he is, keepin' guard."

Jeff knew his face was reddening and was grateful for the dark. He sat up straighter and gripped the Kentucky rifle across his knees. The three veteran trappers lay down one by one, and soon the night was silent except for an occasional snore. After another hour the boy decided his stint was over. He roused his father quietly and went to his own blanket.

Still weary from the long chase he slept like a log. It was the sudden crash of a rifle shot in the gray time before dawn that woke him. He rolled over, clutched his gun, and scrambled to his feet. Through the low-lying mist that came off the river he could see movement—running men and jostling, snorting ponies.

Quick as he had been, there were others ahead of him as he raced toward the horse herd. Another rifle cracked and then another. Eerily out of the mist rang a war whoop that chilled his blood, and he didn't have to be told that it came from an Indian's throat. He heard the sharp *whish* of an arrow past his head, and in the same instant there was a grunt of pain behind him.

Jeff didn't stop to look back. He lifted his rifle and tried to take aim at a naked Cheyenne. The Indian had clawed his way to the back of a rearing pony, but before he was fairly astride, another rifle barked and he toppled off.

Jeff's gun was still cocked when he caught sight of his father, locked in a struggle with a tall red warrior. They grappled hand to hand, with Barlow's useless rifle cast aside. Then from nowhere another Indian appeared. He swung a long-handled, heavy flint ax—the weapon called a warhawk—and his target was the head of Jeff's father. The boy had a split second to stop him. He fired from the hip, dropping the Cheyenne in his tracks.

With shaking hands he tried to reload the rifle, but before he could ram the bullet home, the fight was over. His father's antagonist lay on his back, stabbed by his own knife.

Pale and panting, Jeff looked around him. From where he stood he could see the bodies of at least four Indians. If there had been others, they must have fled into the woods. Close at hand, the mountain men were calmly reloading their guns. Jeff remembered the arrow then. He turned and saw Wind River Slim sitting on the ground, a grin twisting his face.

"Wagh!" the old man grunted. "Anybody goin' to help git this yer arrer out o' me?"

For the first time Jeff saw the feathered shaft protruding from below Slim's collarbone. Shocked, he stumbled toward the wounded trapper, but his father reached him first.

"Go ahead, Jawn," said Slim, "yank her out."

Barlow knelt beside him and studied the position of the arrow. "It's going to hurt some," he said. "But I don't think

it's in a vital spot. Too high to get the life, I reckon. Fitz—come here and help me hold him."

"Shucks!" Slim growled. "No call to hold this hoss!"

But Fitzpatrick stepped behind him and gripped his bony shoulders. John Barlow took hold of the shaft. With one swift, powerful tug he pulled the arrowhead out of the wound. Slim made no sound, but Jeff could see that his teeth were clenched and sweat poured from his forehead.

"Fetch me a beaver pelt," said Fitzpatrick. "An' somethin' we kin use fer a bandage."

Jeff hurried to the nearest pack of fur, not asking whose it was. He pulled out a skin, then snatched a piece of clean cotton shirt he had saved from his "possible" sack. In a moment he was back with them. Fitzpatrick's big hands deftly ripped some of the soft under fur from the pelt and laid it on the ugly red hole in Slim's chest. Then he tore a long strip from the shirt material and bound it tightly over the wound.

"That oughta fix ye, hoss," he told the old hunter with a grin. "Beaver fur's the best thing thar is to stop bleedin'. Reckon ye'll be fitten to ride inside of a week."

Slim gave a snort. "We're headin' out today, like we planned," he replied. "This ain't nothin' but a scratch. How 'bout some breakfast?"

He winked at Jeff, shifted his weight to his good arm, and lifted his gawky frame till he could stagger to his feet. Some of the cooking fires had already been started, and a tempting aroma of coffee was in the air. Jeff hadn't smelled coffee since they left the Platte. It made him suddenly hungry, and he went along with Slim to the nearest fire, where strips of meat were already sizzling.

By noon that day he had helped his father and Pete get part of their fur out of the cache and load the pack ponies. Slim insisted he was able to travel, so, shortly after the noon meal, the whole party started westward, driving the loose horses ahead of them.

Jeff's first sick reaction at having killed a man had worn off by that time. Unlike most of the mountain men he still thought of an Indian as a human being. But whether this one had been white or red, he knew that shooting him was the only way he could have saved his father's life. He hoped such a need would never arise again. To the rest of the trappers that morning's skirmish had been no more than an incident in the day's work. Except for Slim's wound they would have forgotten it. Several of them had complimented Jeff on his quickness and good aim, and Bill Sublette suggested that he keep the Cheyenne warhawk as a memento.

"I reckon ye don't hanker fer his scalp," the older man told him. "Ha'r is messy stuff to tote around anyhow. But this ax is jest as good, an' ye never kin tell—might come in handy some time."

Sublette was riding in the lead, and Barlow and Fitzpatrick acted as a rear guard. Jeff and Slim were up toward the head of the cavalcade. The old trapper sat slouched in his saddle, and Jeff could see that every jolt gave him a twinge of pain. But his lined face was calm, and he never complained.

The river grew smaller as they went up the rocky trail. Every mile they traveled made the great white peaks loom higher in the west. They were only three days away from the South Pass now.

That night they made their last camp on the Sweetwater. In the morning they left the dwindling watercourse and struck northwestward on a trail that became rougher and more difficult hour by hour. It skirted the edges of sheer cliffs and crossed steep slopes of loose, treacherous shale.

Water was no problem, for they encountered hundreds of icy rivulets, carrying off the melting snows. They were far above timber line now. The air was thin—so thin that the horses panted constantly. After a while the men went afoot, leading their mounts. Jeff found himself sucking in deep breaths in an effort to get enough oxygen into his lungs. Only Slim continued to ride, for though he wouldn't admit it, he was too weak to walk.

There was little game at that altitude. They had left the buffalo and the elk, the deer and the antelope far below in the valleys and plains. Sometimes they caught glimpses of distant bighorn sheep, and once, far up on a snowy crag, Jeff saw a Rocky Mountain goat, almost invisible against the white background.

They made a cold camp that second night, for there was no wood big enough to burn. The horses fared better than their riders. They munched on the sparse spring grass while the men had to content themselves with jerky. They slept huddled under buffalo robes.

When Jeff woke, the sun was still behind the eastern mountains. But as he looked around in the faint pink of dawn, he saw that the slope on which they lay was bright with alpine flowers, growing among the boulders and snow patches. Shivering, the men rose, packed their robes and blankets, caught up the horses, and went on again. They were still climbing. As he plodded upward, Jeff had to call on all his reserves to keep his stiff legs moving.

Then at last they could see a broad gap between the peaks a long way ahead. The ground began to level off and walking became easier. Suddenly they were looking out over a tremendous sweep of lower country—dark green forests and rolling mountains that stretched away for hundreds of miles to higher ranges, dim in the distance.

"Thar she is!" shouted Sublette, and a ragged cheer went up from the rest of the mountain men.

The descent on the west side of the pass was steeper than the eastern approach. They went down a thousand feet in less than a mile, riding their horses now. Soon they were down to timber line once more and breathing became easier. Once or twice the trail made a detour around cliffs too steep to negotiate, but before noon they reached a wooded canyon with running water where they could camp and build a fire.

Jeff went to help Slim down from his horse. As he came alongside, he was shocked at the old hunter's appearance. His gaunt face was gray and drawn, and he swayed in the saddle, his eyes closed.

"Hey—Pa!" the boy cried. "Give me a hand with Slim. He looks mighty sick!"

They laid him on a blanket under a lodgepole pine. Fitzpatrick came and looked at him and felt his pulse. Then he opened his shirt. The bandage was dark with dried blood.

"He's too weak to go on," said Fitz soberly. "Shouldn't ha' let him start so soon. Two days o' climbin' with nothin' much to eat was too hard on him. We'd better put on some more fur an' a new bandage, an' then give him some broth if he'll drink it. Meantime, I'll go after fresh meat."

He mounted and set off at once. Inside of an hour he was back with a blacktail doe across his saddle. Jeff and his father had cooked up some soup made of jerked meat, but after a swallow or two Slim shook his head and refused to take any more.

"Tastes like ye'd made it out of an old moccasin," he murmured, and tried to grin.

The venison was quickly roasted, and they brought him the choicest pieces. They watched his valiant effort to eat a few mouthfuls. Then he lay back again, closing his eyes. Fitz shook his head and turned away.

"I figgered that'd fetch him," he said in a low voice. "If he ain't hongry fer fresh deer liver, I'm feared he's in a bad way."

Jeff and his father covered their old friend with a blanket, for it was cold there in the shade, even in the middle of the day. For the next two hours they sat beside him while one mountain man after another came silently over to look at the invalid. Nobody even thought of going any farther that afternoon.

After a time Jeff saw the long body quiver, and Slim coughed convulsively. From the side of his mouth a line of bright red blood dribbled down the stubbly chin. John Barlow got up quickly and went to call Fitzpatrick. Jeff could hear them talking when they returned.

"Guess I was wrong about that arrow," his father said. "It must have hit the upper part o' the lung. He's bleeding inside."

They knelt down beside him and Fitz laid a gentle hand over the bony old wrist, feeling for the pulse. Slim opened his eyes.

"This coon," he whispered, "ain't a-goin' to make it to the rendezvous. When ye git thar, Fitz, drink a couple fer me."

He paused a moment, struggling for breath. Then he spoke again, so hoarsely they could barely hear the words. "Want my beaver," he panted, "to go to the boy here. Reckon if he has the chance, he'll be a mighty good painter some day."

Again his eyes closed and a little smile twitched at the corners of his mouth. Before they realized it, he was gone.

chapter 15

That evening they buried Slim among the trees, there on the western slope of the Continental Divide. John Barlow read a short passage from the Bible—the psalm that began "I will lift up mine eyes unto the hills." Fitzpatrick and Bill Sublette, who had been his oldest friends, spoke briefly. Their words came stumbling but from the heart.

"It's sort o' fittin'," said Fitz, "fer him to lay here alongside the trail. Thar wa'n't nobody had more to do with findin' it than Slim. Might say it was him that opened up the way to the West."

Pete LeBlanc stood there with tears rolling down his rugged face. "He was a good man," he said brokenly. "I geev beaver to church—burn plenty candles for heem."

All working together they moved a big rock to the top of the grave, and Jeff's father chipped out letters on its flat face. "Wind River Slim," the crude inscription read. "Mountain Man. Died April 28, 1828."

"Anybody know what his real name was?" Barlow asked, but they all shook their heads.

"Reckon he'd like it better this way," Bill Sublette replied.

Early next morning they loaded the horses and were on

their way again. The trail led downward gradually till, late in the afternoon, they reached the banks of a stream flowing to the southwest. There Sublette ordered his men to make camp.

"This yer's the Sandy," Jeff heard him say. "A ways down she runs into the Siskeedee—that's the Injun name fer the Green. Ye kin see thar's been hosses through in the last week. Pack hosses, I'd jedge from the tracks. Could be Shoshones, bringin' their fur to the rendezvous."

They kept a horse guard that night, and the next morning Fitzpatrick and Jeff's father rode out to scout their back trail. Two hours later John Barlow came back alone.

"We sighted a big party o' white men coming through the pass," he reported. "Fitz went on to meet 'em. He's pretty sure it's LaCasse with the trade goods."

Raoul LaCasse, Jeff had heard, was the *bourgeois*—pronounced "burgeway" by the mountain men—who would handle the trading with Indians and trappers. It was also his job to see that the fur got safely to St. Louis, for he was one of General Ashley's righthand men.

The camp waited eagerly. Every few minutes one trapper or another would climb the rise behind them to look eastward. At last they heard singing—lusty French voices raised in an old song of the *voyageurs*. And down the trail from the eastward came a long train of men and horses. Somebody fired off a welcoming gun and then the valley popped with shots like firecrackers.

Within a few minutes the bank of the Sandy was alive with traders and trappers. There must have been twenty-five men in LaCasse's party, and more than twice that many horses, loaded with trade goods. There was an immediate celebration. Everywhere Jeff heard boisterous greetings, shouts, and laughter. Sadly he thought of Slim and how he would have enjoyed it all.

The men clamored for liquor, but LaCasse firmly refused to open any casks. "You boys have got to stay sober till we reach the Green," he told them. "Once we get the rendezvous set up, you're welcome to celebrate till your beaver's gone."

Sublette and Fitzpatrick backed him up. The newly arrived ponies were given a chance to rest. Then, after two hours, the whole cavalcade moved southwest again.

* * * *

It was on the second morning after the traders joined them that they came to a larger river—the fast-flowing Siskeedee itself. The bank was lined with cottonwoods, but back of them lay a broad, flat meadow, green with good grass and bright with flowers. This was the place chosen for the rendezvous.

Already there were two small camps of Indians there. The tepees rose white in the sun, and dogs and children ran everywhere while the squaws went about their work.

The men—Shoshones in one village and Piutes in the other—squatted at ease in front of their lodges, talking and smoking their pipes.

The French *engagés* in LaCasse's party were good workers. As soon as they had finished unloading the horses and picketing them, they set about building the trading post. A dozen men went into the woods with their axes and worked like beavers felling trees. The rest shaped the logs and put up the walls.

Meanwhile, the hunters had gone out after fresh meat. Jeff and his father ranged eastward into the hills and found the blacktail deer abundant. Before sundown they rode back to camp with a buck apiece. They kept enough meat for themselves and turned over the rest to the common larder.

The weather had been fine for several days. Now clouds were gathering and there was a threat of rain that kept the LaCasse men working far into the night. Before the first drops began to fall, they had raised all four walls and roofed their structure with poles. Over these they slung big tarpaulins, brought along for the purpose. The trade goods were carried inside and safely stored.

The two Barlows had picked their own campsite as soon as they arrived. It was on a little rise of ground, sheltered by trees. There they threw up a pole lean-to, covered it with a couple of buffalo robes, and soon had a snug sleeping place, protected from the wet.

The rain continued most of the following day. Meanwhile, the camp grew in size. Small groups of trappers came straggling in with their season's catch. By late afternoon, when the clouds broke at last, the trading-post building was full of revelers. It was a fairly large cabin, some thirty feet wide and twenty deep. There were two doors, and a long counter ran from end to end with the bales of trade goods behind it. Indians were supposed to use one door and one end of the counter while the white trappers stayed in the other half.

In theory, at least, trade whisky was doled out only to the white men. The government in Washington had taken a strong stand against supplying liquor to Indians. However, Washington was a long way from this little-known mountain country, and many of the trappers took advantage of the fact. They would trade two or three beaver for a jug of whisky, mix it with water, and sell it to thirsty Piutes at outrageous prices. Jeff saw a prime pelt handed over by an Indian in exchange for a single tin cupful of the diluted stuff.

Many of the squaws accompanied their men to the store, anxious to get blankets, beads, and other wanted articles before the beaver skins were squandered on liquor. It took very little to make an Indian drunk. After one or two good swigs a brave was likely to stagger around with a foolish grin, give a few hiccuping whoops, and sprawl on the ground to sleep while his faithful squaw watched over him.

As the number of white men at the rendezvous increased, the din grew louder. Night and day they drank and sang, fired off their guns in the air, gambled and wrestled and fought.

On the third evening Fitzpatrick strolled over to the Barlow camp.

"I see you ain't much fer celebratin', John," he said with a laugh. "Hope they don't keep ye awake all night. I git a leetle sick o' the commotion myself after a spell. Too bad ol' Slim ain't here, though. He allus liked it fine."

He turned to Jeff then. "Slim 'peared to think quite a lot o' you, boy," he said. "Tol' me you painted picters. Got any of 'em handy that I could see?"

Flattered, Jeff undid the bundle in which he had packed

his paintings. As he unrolled one skin after another, Fitz's eyes widened. He stared at the pictures and made excited comments.

"Durn' if I can't fair hear that buffler beller!" he said delightedly. "Who's the Crow hunter killin' the bull?"

Jeff described their meeting with White Calf's band and the buffalo hunt. "The one on the pony is Running Wolf," he said. "This other picture is of old White Calf himself. He was a long-time friend o' Slim's."

The famous mountain man was beaming. "Know what ye'd oughta do, boy?" he said. "Draw a picter o' Wind River Slim whilst he's still fresh in yore memory."

The same thought had been in Jeff's mind. "I'd like to try it," he answered eagerly. "It'll take some time to cure another skin, but soon as I've got one, I'll do my best."

"Jest wait here," Fitz commanded, and stalked off into the night. He was back in ten or fifteen minutes with a beautiful pale-tanned deer hide. "Bought her cheap from a Shoshone squaw," he announced. "You paint Slim's likeness an' I'll give ye five plew fer it."

* * * *

As the days passed, trading went on briskly. The burgeway rubbed his hands and greeted each newly arrived trapper jovially. He was a big bull of a man, paunchy now, but powerfully built. From his father, Jeff had learned a little of LaCasse's history.

The story went that he was only a dozen years old when he started in the fur trade. Born in Quebec, he had run away and joined a fur brigade headed for the West. The first year they had reached Fort Detroit. Later they pushed on to Mackinac and all the way to the upper end of Lake Superior, trading with the Chippewa and other northern Indians. When he was sixteen, LaCasse had set out alone from the headwaters of the Mississippi, paddling south in a canoe. Captured by a roving band of Sioux, he had spent two years learning the ways of the tribe. Then he had escaped and made his way downriver to St. Louis.

The only languages he knew up to that time were French and a few Indian dialects. Many people in St. Louis spoke French, and one of them gave the husky youth a job in a blacksmith shop. But that didn't satisfy him. He applied himself to learning English, then bookkeeping. Within three years he not only spoke and wrote English fluently, but he had also earned a position as accountant for a wealthy fur merchant.

Through hard work, honesty, and a keen knowledge of the Indians, Raoul LaCasse went on to become one of the most successful traders in St. Louis. General Ashley was known for his daring and enthusiasm, but many said it was LaCasse who had kept the Rocky Mountain Fur Company a solid money-making concern.

Ten days after the trading started, practically all the free trappers within a radius of five hundred miles were present or accounted for. They came in from every point of the compass. Some had wintered on the Green, the Salmon, and the Snake, west of the Divide. Others had trapped along the Big Horn or in the "valley of stinking smokes," at the foot of the Grand Teton. And there were a few who had worked the headwaters of the South Platte and the Arkansas in the shadow of the Sangre de Cristo Range.

Three men were reported missing, and nobody at the rendezvous had any doubts that they were dead. They had gone into the rich fur country between the Big Horn and the Yellowstone—a rash move because that was known to be Blackfoot territory.

Fitzpatrick shook his head when he heard about them. "I've tangled with Blackfeet once or twice," he said, "an' I'm plumb lucky to have my ha'r. Their dog soldiers are the proudest, toughest fighters in the hull Nor'west. A Blackfoot won't trade or parley with any white man, an' mighty few of 'em ever touch liquor."

LaCasse kept the rendezvous going for a full two weeks. Then, when all the fur in the district had been bought and the trade goods were exhausted, he gave the word to his Frenchmen to strike camp. The night before they were to start eastward, the burgeway came over to the Barlows' fire. He accepted a cup of coffee and sat down on a log.

"Trading all done?" Jeff's father asked.

LaCasse nodded. "We'll pull stakes in the morning. Had a good season. General Ashley ought to be good an' happy when he sees what we've taken. There'll be close to three hundred packs."

John Barlow whistled. "How you going to carry all that fur?" he asked.

"Well," the burgeway told him, "we brought in about fifty ponies. Traded with the Piutes for twenty more, but that still leaves us short. Didn't I hear you had some spare horses you might want to sell?"

"Could be," Jeff's father replied noncommittally. "We took a few from the Cheyennes that tried to rob us. How much do you figure to pay?"

"Round three plew is the price for Injun ponies, if they're sound."

"These are saddle stock—war ponies—strong and well-fed. Seems as if four plew a head would be about right."

They continued the friendly bargaining for twenty minutes, then settled on a compromise of three-and-a-half plew each for twelve horses. No beaver pelts actually changed hands, of course. The money, amounting to over $250, would be credited to John Barlow's account in St. Louis.

LaCasse stood up as if to leave, then turned to Jeff. "One other thing I might consider trading for," he said. "Fitzpatrick says you've drawn some pictures. Mind if I see what they're like?"

Proudly Jeff brought out his deerskin paintings. The burgeway studied them, looking longest at the new picture of Wind River Slim. Jeff knew it was good. He had put his heart in it, and the old mountain man's lined face on the deerskin almost seemed ready to speak.

"How much you want for that one?" LaCasse asked.

Jeff shook his head. "It's not for sale," he replied. "I did it for Fitz."

LaCasse went over the others and offered two plew apiece for the lot. But John Barlow merely laughed.

"I reckon they'll be worth a bit more in St. Louis," he said. "Jeff and I are going downriver with you if you can use some spare hands. A couple o' good rifles might be a help, if you should need meat or run afoul of Indians."

"Fine!" LaCasse replied with pleasure. "Maybe the boy'll see new things to draw on the voyage. Bring your ponies down early. We'll be on our way before noon."

When he had left, Jeff turned eagerly to his father. "Is that right, Pa?" he asked. "Are we really going downriver in the keelboats?"

Barlow puffed at his pipe and nodded. "I aim to take you to the city, and I don't think we'll be coming back. Like I told you back in Illinois, I wanted you to have a year in the mountains with Slim and me before the country was spoiled. I reckon it did you some good, too. But it'll never be quite the same again.

"Sure—I know there are plenty o' hidden places like the one we found, where the beaver are still thick. But one after another they're being trapped out. There aren't many o' the old-time mountain men left, now that Slim's gone. And there'll be more and more tenderfeet coming this way, killing off the game and stirring up trouble with the Indians. In another few years there'll be movers sweating across the mountains in wagons, heading for Oregon. That'll be the end o' the life you and I've seen."

"Wagons?" Jeff asked in a tone of disbelief. "I'd like to see any wagon try to come over the South Pass!"

"Don't bet against it," his father told him. "You'd be surprised at what land-hungry folks can do if they set out to. Down at Independence they're already talking about making up whole trains of wagons and heading west. A lot of 'em are bound to die trying, but there'll be more that get through. After a while you'll see a regular trail all the way to the Columbia River."

chapter **16**

After breakfast next morning they loaded their belongings on two pack ponies, mounted their saddle horses, and drove the rest of the herd over to the main camp. The French *engagés* were busy packing up the fur.

The Barlows had turned over their own pelts to LaCasse the week before and purchased such necessities as powder and bullets. Also they had indulged in a few luxuries. Coffee and sugar were among these, and Jeff's father had treated himself to a bar of soap and a new razor.

Nearly all the mountain men prided themselves on being clean-shaven. At least, they shaved once a week. As a rule, they performed this rite with cold water and a well-honed hunting knife. Jeff was glad his own cheeks were still smooth. He had often shuddered at the sight of old Slim scraping away at his gray bristles. John Barlow, however, had carried a razor ever since he came to the mountains. He kept it sharp by stropping it on his moccasin sole.

Hair was another matter. Jeff's dark mane now hung all the way to his shoulders, and so did his father's. All winter they had kept their bodies clean by taking baths in water heated over the cook fire, and since they reached the Siskeedee, Jeff had gone swimming nearly every day in the clear, fast-flowing river.

By midmorning the Indians had broken camp and were trailing off in various directions, their skin tepees folded and carried on *travois* made of the lodgepoles. The squaws, children, and dogs trotted along beside the pack horses, while the braves rode in the lead.

Singing lustily as they worked, the fur company men lashed the last of the packs aboard the ponies. There was much shouting in French, up and down the line. Then LaCasse, mounted on a big gray horse, waved his arm.

"Allons!" he bellowed, and the whole long cavalcade began to move.

There were thirty or forty free trappers in the party, heading east over the divide. Most of them would go back to their favorite hunting grounds, and Bill Sublette had already started on an expedition to the Snake. A few others, like the Barlows, planned to make the trip to St. Louis. The mountain men kept to themselves, scornful of their noisy French fellow travelers.

All afternoon they climbed, and at sunset camp was made on the higher slopes beside the Sandy. Fitzpatrick left his own fire to come over for a chat with the Barlows.

"Know how much fur thar was in that lot Slim left ye?" he asked Jeff. "I talked to the burgeway an' he says it'll come to more'n forty plew—right 'round two hunderd an' fifty dollars. I understan' thar's some more cached down on the Sweetwater, too. Looks like you'll be one o' the richest young'uns in St. Louis!"

"He's going to need all of it, I reckon," John Barlow surprised his son by saying. "If he wants to be an artist, I figure he ought to learn to be a good one. So I aim to take him east—maybe all the way to Philadelphia."

"Gosh, Pa!" Jeff cried. "Honest—you mean it?"

"Yes," said his father. "You've had enough rough living

to last you awhile. Now it's time you got back to civilized ways—learned how to act around city folks and women and children. I reckon a year or two more of school wouldn't hurt, along with studying art."

Jeff's excitement ebbed away when he heard those last words. He supposed going back to school was a necessary evil, but he had begun to think of himself as a full-grown man. After all, he had survived a Rocky Mountain winter, killed his share of game, and trapped his share of fur.

Fitz saw the boy's face fall and smiled. "Schoolin' never hurt a man," he remarked. "Look at yore paw. I reckon Wind River Slim would be proud to know you was spendin' some o' his fur on eddication."

* * * *

They reached the South Pass at last and crossed over to the eastern slope. The thin air of the heights was easier to take than it had been when they came up in the opposite direction. Moving downhill, the horses made good time, and the men could ride instead of walking. After four days they reached the little stream they knew was the upper Sweetwater.

Now that they were below the timber line, good grass was abundant. The little river teemed with trout. The group of hunters, led by Fitzpatrick and the two Barlows, rode out in the late afternoon and were back before sunset with fresh-killed deer and elk. Around the fires the big camp ate, drank, joked, and sang.

With more than a hundred horses in the herd, it was necessary to keep them guarded at night. Jeff took his turn with the others, alert for possible Indian raids, but they were unmolested. The trip down the Sweetwater trail went smoothly, and they soon reached the cliff where they had cached their fur.

It was here that Pete LeBlanc took leave of them. He and

two other trappers planned to cross to the Popo Agie and wait there for the fall trapping. Jeff was sorry to see him go, for he had become fond of the burly Frenchman.

They got their furs out of the cache, packed them on ponies, and the procession set out eastward again. Another four days of travel brought them to the confluence of the Sweetwater and the North Platte.

"A few seasons back," Fitzpatrick told Jeff, as they rode together down the trail, "thar was a couple o' fellers tried to take their beaver down from here in bullboats."

He chuckled to himself, and the boy waited for him to go on. "What happened?" he asked finally.

"Wal," said the mountain man, "they made out fine fer the fust twenty mile or so. Then they hit white water, an' the boats spun around till the trappers was plumb dizzy. Pretty soon the river went over a fall. They managed to swim ashore, but the water fer miles was full o' packs o' fur. What they managed to save was mebbe a third o' their catch, an' their rifles was gone, too. Must ha' made a pretty sorry sight, settin' thar in wet buckskins on the bank."

Jeff's father had ridden up in time to hear the last part of the story. "That's right." He laughed. "They were a sorry sight, sure enough. By the time we found you, Fitz, you and Slim had used up all the cuss words you knew."

"Shucks!" said Fitzpatrick sheepishly. "Ye had no call to tell him who the durn fools was, John."

This was the same country Jeff had seen the previous fall, but it looked different now, as they moved eastward. Grass and trees were still green with the freshness of early summer, and birds sang in the cottonwood groves. At evening he saw young fawns coming to the riverbank with their mothers to drink. They were pretty things, and he never thought of harming them. There were plenty of grown animals when meat was needed. The day after they passed the mouth of the Casper, they sighted buffalo. It wasn't a big herd, but the hunters brought in a young bull and two cows —enough food for a week's traveling. By the time it was gone they had reached Scott's Bluffs.

From that point on the North Platte was somewhat easier to navigate, and it was there that LaCasse had left his keelboats. There were two of the flat-bottomed, square-ended craft pulled up on shore. Ten French rivermen had been left to guard them, and eight still remained. What had happened to the other two was a mystery. All their companions knew was that they had gone out on the two ponies they had, looking for buffalo. They had never come back.

"Did ye see any sign of Injuns?" Fitzpatrick asked, but the *engagés* shook their heads.

"Could be that same bunch o' Cheyennes that tangled with us," John Barlow suggested. "They were afoot, but they probably made it this far on their way home. And they'd have done almost anything to get horses. Let's ride out a way and see what we can find."

Jeff rode with Fitz and his father. The trail was more than two weeks old, but the mountain men succeeded in following it, dismounting now and then to puzzle out the faint tracks. Five miles from the river they found old buffalo sign. Then, a little farther on they came to the skeleton of a good-sized bull.

"They shot him an' was likely skinnin' him out," said Fitz. "Injuns snuck up on 'em an' grabbed the hosses. Yep, this could be a moccasin track. My guess is we'll find 'em not too fur off."

They could make out horse tracks leading off to the east, but instead of following them, Fitz pointed to a grove of small trees a short distance away. "John," he said, "if'n you was goin' to hide a couple o' bodies, wouldn't you pick a place like yon?"

They rode to the grove and tethered the ponies, going

in on foot. Jeff was halfway through a patch of brush when he saw the glimmer of whitened bones. Shocked, he stood still a moment, then called to his father.

"Pa," he said, his voice shaking, "I reckon this is where they are."

The two older men parted the bushes. The skeletons lay close together, a few shreds of clothing under the stripped bones.

"Took their ha'r an' their guns," growled Fitz, "an' left 'em here fer the wolves. Trail's too old now, but this coon'd shore like to ketch up with the varmints that done it."

They gathered the bones together in a saddle blanket and carried them back to the camp. There was no priest with the LaCasse party, but the burgeway had a Catholic prayer book, and he read a burial service over the hastily dug graves. Afterward the men set about calking the boats and dragging them to the water. By the following morning the furs and supplies were packed aboard, and the flotilla was ready to cast off.

Jeff had never had a close look at a keelboat before. Each craft was about fifty feet long and twelve feet wide, solidly built of oak planking. At either end there was a decked-over space, but the whole middle section was an open cargo hold, covered only by tarpaulins. Along each gunwale ran a foot-wide walkway, on which the boatmen moved while poling upstream. The vessel was steered by a broad sweep oar, set in chocks in the stern. On the forward deck of one boat a two-pounder swivel gun was mounted.

The French creoles who manned the boats were a happy lot. Coming upriver had been back-breaking work all the way. Now they were headed home, with the current to help them, and not even the death of their two comrades could long dampen their spirits. They pushed out from the bank to the tune of a jolly river song and were soon swinging along southeastward, pushed by the hurrying water.

The six men assigned as hunters rode along the shore parallel to the river, driving the horse herd. Usually they could keep the boats in sight, but if not, it made little difference. They knew LaCasse would tie up at an appointed spot to wait for their arrival.

Jeff and his father were among the group of hunters, all mountain men, led by Fitzpatrick. Most of the time four riders kept the horses moving while two scouted ahead, looking for signs of game or Indians.

It was the third day below Scott's Bluffs, in the stretch between Chimney Rock and Courthouse Rock, that they found buffalo. The two Barlows had ridden out in the lead that morning, ranging several miles to the south of the river. On their right there were bare, flat-topped hills, too low to be called buttes but high enough to hide the plain beyond.

"What say we ride up there and reconnoiter?" said Jeff's father. "There's a haze in the sky that might be dust."

They rode to within a few yards of the rim, then dismounted and went toward the top on foot. John Barlow knelt down, took off his hat, and eased himself upward till he could see over. After a moment he beckoned to Jeff to come up and join him. As he looked out over the expanse of plain, the boy's breath caught in his throat.

As far as the eye could see, there were buffalo—thousands upon thousands of them—moving slowly across the landscape toward the river. They walked at a leisurely pace or stopped to graze as they pleased. From the vast, dark sea of animals came a continuous sound, made up of the bleating of calves and the gentle mooing of their mothers. Occasionally a bull gave his rumbling bellow.

In the distance, behind the enormous herd, Jeff could see slinking gray shapes that he knew were wolves. They were following hungrily, waiting for strays or sick animals to become separated from the main body.

"Ride back," Barlow told his son, "and tell Fitz. He'll want to send a couple more hunters and some ponies to carry the meat. I'll wait here for you."

Jeff knew the buckskin pony had scented the herd, for his ears were up and his nostrils flaring eagerly. He kicked the horse into action and set off down the slope at a dead run. The other men saw him coming. Before he was within hailing distance, Fitzpatrick was riding out to meet him.

"Trouble, boy?" he asked.

"No," Jeff panted. "Big herd o' buffalo. If you can spare some men, we've got a chance to kill a lot o' meat."

Within a few minutes Fitz and another hunter had cut half a dozen horses out of the herd, put lead ropes on them, and were galloping in Jeff's wake. Soon they cleared the rise and saw the dark mass of buffalo blanketing the plain. They joined John Barlow.

"Jeff," his father told the boy, "somebody's got to stay back and hold the pack horses. I guess you're elected. Don't bring 'em near the herd until we give you a signal."

Jeff was bitterly disappointed, but he didn't argue. He knew the shooting should be done by the most experienced men. He gathered up the ropes and led the ponies forward at a walk, while the others rode toward the flank of the herd, half a mile away.

The great dust cloud thickened and rose higher till it nearly obscured the sun. The buffalo, Jeff saw, were no longer moving at a walk. They were running, and the noise they made was like the roar of thunder. Joined to the bellowing and squalling was the earth-shaking thud of countless hoofs.

He was wondering what had started them stampeding when he heard another sound—a shrill, high-pitched yell-

ing that came from the west. And through the dust he caught a glimpse of distant men on horseback. Indians—riding close on the heels of the galloping herd!

Jeff knew his ponies, moving slowly along the skyline, would be in plain sight of the red hunters if they looked in his direction. Within half a minute he was pulling the horses over the rim of the low butte, where they would be hidden. Once there, he quickly swung out of the saddle, tied the lead ropes to the pommel, and stood behind his buckskin, the Kentucky rifle held ready.

It was well that he did, for almost at that instant two Indians came over the crest at a dead run. They leaned low over their ponies' necks, the short, heavy buffalo bows in their hands. And when they caught sight of him, they let out a blood-curdling yell that made him tremble. Nevertheless, he stood firm, teeth clenched, his rifle sights steady on the first of the attackers.

The Indian was riding a pinto pony. He raced down the slope at breakneck speed till Jeff could see the whites of the horse's rolling eyes. Still the boy held his fire. And at the last possible second the rider swerved away. He slipped out of sight on the far side of the pinto and yelled something to the second Indian before he reappeared. Then, to Jeff's amazement, they both came to a halt a few yards away and held their bows over their heads in a sign of peace. It was only then that the boy realized he was looking into the grinning face of Chief White Calf's son, Running Wolf.

chapter 17

Jeff lowered his rifle and stepped out to meet the pair. That pinto horse had looked familiar when it first came over the hill, but there were many ponies marked that way among the Plains tribes. Now he could recognize the lithe young figure in the feather headdress that he had drawn in his picture of the hunt.

Pointing southward over the rim, he tried to explain in sign language what he was doing here. Running Wolf seemed to understand. He nodded, grinned again, and dashed off up the hill with his companion. As they disappeared beyond the crest, Jeff heard the distant bark of rifles. Once more he led the pack horses to the top of the butte and urged them after the fleeing buffalo.

Far off to the eastward he could hear continued firing from the white men's Hawken guns. Then it stopped. Above the bellowing of the herd the only sounds now were the frenzied whoops of the Crow hunters.

Pulling the ponies along as fast as they would go, Jeff at last caught up with stragglers from the herd. He was tempted to take a shot at a fat young cow, but when he saw that she was heavy with calf, he held his fire. Then something else caught his attention.

Less than half a mile ahead, the frantic buffalo were disappearing over the rim of the butte. Off to one side he could see the three white hunters sitting still on their horses. Meanwhile, the Indians rode on, shouting and waving their blankets to keep the herd from turning. A sick feeling came to the boy's stomach. He advanced reluctantly, dreading what he was going to see.

As he neared the rim, the last big surge of buffalo plunged over it, out of sight. And the triumphant yell of the Crow dog soldiers told him he had been right. The edge of the butte was a terrible trap. Here on the west it fell away steeply in a forty-foot cliff. Jeff's father called to him to keep away, but he had to see for himself. He rode toward the edge, took one look at the struggling mass of brown bodies below, and was glad to turn back.

"Come on," said John Barlow gruffly. "We've got our own skinning to do. Bring the horses."

"Yer paw's right," Fitz told him. "What's goin' on down thar ain't a fit sight fer white men. It's enough to turn yer stummick."

Back along the plain they came to the first of half a dozen dead buffalo shot by the mountain men. Working in pairs, they flayed off the hides and methodically cut away the better parts of the meat. Within an hour the pack ponies were loaded with all they could carry.

"John," said Fitzpatrick, "you an' the others better take this meat back to the river. Me—I aim to have a talk with Runnin' Wolf. See if he feels like buyin' a bunch o' hosses."

As they rode northward, Jeff asked his father some questions. "When the Indians run all those buffalo over a cliff," he said, "don't they kill a lot more'n they can use?"

His father gave a grim nod. "They figure," he replied, "there's no end to the herds. I've heard white men talk the same way. But they're wrong. There'll be fewer buffalo every year—finally none at all."

"How many do you think they killed in that stampede?" Jeff asked.

"At least a hundred, counting those with broken legs. The bulk of 'em got away, trampling on the bodies of the first ones. A drive like that's a brutal business, son. I'm sorry you had to see it."

* * * *

Three days later the hunting party overtook the keelboats. LaCasse had tied up just above the mouth of the South Platte. He welcomed the buffalo meat they had brought and was still more pleased at the news Fitzpatrick gave him. The Crows had taken most of the horse herd, agreeing to send more meat and buffalo robes and to return the ponies to LaCasse's men when they came upriver the following spring.

It was another twenty-four hours before Running Wolf and his braves appeared. They brought the skins and meat as promised, and that night a feast was held in their honor. It was well to have at least one friendly tribe along the route of the fur brigades. Presents were showered on the chief's son. Then LaCasse and Fitzpatrick made flowery speeches in the Indian tongue and toasted the Crow nation in trade whisky. Everybody was late getting to bed, but at dawn the next morning the burgeway was routing out his sleepy Frenchmen.

After an early breakfast the boats pulled out into the current. Stubby masts had been set up amidships, and each boat carried a square sail that now filled to a fair wind.

The scouts had kept their own horses and two or three pack ponies. As the boats departed, they set off down the right bank, and a few minutes later they started the long swim across the South Platte. Jeff, on his buckskin, followed the course set by Fitzpatrick and his father. In many places the river was shallow enough to touch bottom, but there were quicksands that made it treacherous. Thanks to the guidance of the old hands they completed the crossing without mishap. Once they got to the other side, they unsaddled the dripping horses and let them roll and rest while they dried out their gear.

"Good thing we got all that buffler meat," Fitz remarked. "Won't be as much game from here on, an' we'll have to keep our eyes peeled fer Injuns. Below Brady's Island we'll be in Pawnee country. Pawnees ain't predictable. Sometimes they're friendly as pups, but if'n somebody's riled 'em up, they kin be plenty mean."

It was still well before noon when they saddled up again. Below the forks the river ran broad and yellow and sluggish, nearly a mile across in places. They put the horses to a trot and covered a few more miles before they stopped to eat. The cottonwoods had disappeared. From here to the Missouri they would have to depend on buffalo chips for fuel, and once more the duty of gathering them fell to Jeff. He grumbled a little, but the chips weren't hard to find. Everywhere along the river the herds had left their droppings, and it was possible to gather an armful of dry dung in ten minutes.

When he climbed the side of a sand hill, he could see the keelboats—two tiny dots in the distance, moving slowly down with the current.

They camped that night a little way below Brady's Island. Thousands of waterfowl flew up from the reeds at Jeff's approach, and he was tempted to try for one with his rifle. His father, however, had warned him not to do any firing as long as they had enough meat. If there were hostile Indians in the neighborhood, they might hear the shots.

It had been hot on the trail that day, but after sunset it turned cooler. Jeff wrapped himself in his blanket and listened to the yapping howl of coyotes, muffled by the sound of the great wind that blew constantly across the plains. Behind him were the dunes—the "coast" of the Platte. And beyond them he knew the rolling prairie unfolded, mile on empty mile to the edge of the world.

He was asleep when his father called him a couple of hours later. "Your turn to stand guard," John Barlow whispered. "Keep awake and keep an eye on the ponies. When that bright star yonder is overhead, you can wake the next man."

Nothing happened during Jeff's watch. He stayed alert, scanning the skyline of the ridge behind their camp, and when the climbing star told him his time was up, he roused one of the other hunters.

Fitzpatrick had chosen the last watch of the night, from four o'clock till sunrise. That was the time when most Indian attacks came—in the uncertain light before dawn. Slim had once told Jeff why this was so. Most of the tribes, he said, were afraid of the evil spirits that walked in the darkness.

Jeff was roused from sleep by the heavy *whang* of a Hawken gun. He rolled to his feet, fumbling for his own rifle. In the gray half-dark the others were up and running past him, but he heard no more shots. Fitz, when they reached him, was casually reloading his rifle.

"Sorry to wake you coons up," he said with a chuckle. "Had to stop an Injun that was crawlin' down after the hosses. Thar was some more with him, but they rid off when I fired."

"You hit him?" Barlow asked.

" 'Fraid so. Jest meant to skeer him, but he stuck his head up at the wrong time."

The mountain man strolled toward the fallen shape, his rifle held ready in case the Indian should still be alive. They saw him turn the body over with his foot.

"Squar' betwixt the eyes," he reported. "A Pawnee, by the ha'r."

Drawn by curiosity, Jeff went to look. The dead savage was naked except for a breechclout and moccasins, but there was a necklace of wolves' teeth around his throat. Unlike the Crows and Sioux and Cheyennes, who wore their hair long, this brave had a roached mane running back from the top of his forehead to his neck.

John Barlow came to stand beside his son, a frown on his face. "Too bad," he said. "This fellow was pretty well up in the tribe. A 'Buffalo with Small Horns,' I'd judge, from the paint and the necklace. Maybe a chief's son. Could be we'll have trouble about him before very long."

Fitzpatrick knew it, too. He was silent at breakfast and got up quickly when he had finished eating. "Douse the fire," he ordered, "an' let's git movin'. I'd like to keep in sight o' the boats."

They pushed the horses hard through the morning. At noon they could barely make out the keelboats in the distance, and after a short rest to water the ponies, they started riding again. Late in the afternoon, where the river made an oxbow to the right, Fitz led them across country by a short cut. They came out on the bank half an hour later and sighted the boats swinging around the bend.

One of the hunters dismounted quickly, unrolled his blanket, and handed it to Fitzpatrick. The veteran leader waved it over his head, steadily, back and forth, until he attracted the attention of the rivermen. They could see LaCasse standing big and burly in his broad-brimmed hat on the foredeck of the nearest craft. At his order the steersman turned the bow toward shore.

"Reckon it's just as well they're coming," said John Barlow quietly. "We've got company."

Over the ridge of the sand hill behind them a score of

riders had appeared, moving at a gallop. Jeff didn't need to look twice to know they were Pawnees, bent on revenge.

"Git down," Fitzpatrick told them. "Tie the hosses together an' fort up behind 'em. Don't anybody shoot till I give the word."

The mountain men moved quickly. In a quarter of a minute they were standing behind the close-bunched ponies, waiting for the charge. The Indians had been sighted from the boats now. Shouted orders came faintly over the water, and when Jeff stole a glance in that direction, he saw men loading the little cannon in the bow.

The Pawnees approached fast, bent low over their horses' necks, and the shrilling of their war whoops was enough to send cold chills down a man's spine. Two or three of the leaders, Jeff saw, were waving guns.

"Steady, son," his father told him. "Don't let those trade muskets scare you. I never saw an Indian yet that could shoot straight with one."

The distance shortened swiftly. When the nearest Pawnees were only thirty yards away, the charge split to either side. A musket banged and arrows whistled past.

"Now!" shouted Fitz. "Let 'em have it!" His shot knocked an Indian to the ground, and one by one the other mountain men fired, picking their targets. Jeff swung his rifle to the left as a red warrior flashed past. Only one leg was visible above the pony's back, but his bullet shattered the kneecap and the Pawnee tumbled off, yelling with pain. As fast as his hands could work, the boy reloaded. He was setting the percussion cap when his father gave a cry of warning.

The second wave of Indians was upon them now. Instead of sheering off, like the first ones, they came straight on, brandishing their wicked-looking buffalo spears. Jeff's buckskin horse screamed horribly and went down, knocking the boy sidewise. He fell in a cloud of dust, still clutching his gun, and the flying hoofs of an Indian pony missed his head by inches.

Dazed, he got to his knees, looking for something to shoot at in the melee around him. The Pawnees had ridden right through the bunched ponies, killing or maiming at least half of them. Now they were circling back for another charge, yelling with triumph. As the dust cleared, Jeff saw that two of the hunters lay wounded.

"You all right, Pa?" he quavered.

"Yep," said John Barlow. "Get ready. They'll be coming again."

He was crouched low behind one of the dead horses, his face calm as he leveled his rifle. As Jeff crawled forward to join him, something whistled overhead and a booming crash came from the river. The swivel gun!

The cannonball struck in the very middle of the attackers, throwing them into confusion. For a moment they circled aimlessly. Then, before the men in the keelboat could reload, the Indians galloped off toward the shelter of the dunes.

Jeff's father got to his feet and went to the nearest of the fallen mountain men. Fitzpatrick was attending to the other. At his father's side, Jeff saw that the wounded hunter's face was pale and blood was staining his buckskin shirt. A spear thrust had caught him in the shoulder.

"Good, clean wound," John Barlow told the man. "We'll get this bleeding stopped and you'll be fine. Jeff—go meet the boats and tell LaCasse to bring bandages."

Running down the bank, Jeff saw that the two keelboats had nosed in among the reeds.

"How bad is it?" called the burgeway.

"Two men got hurt," the boy answered, "an' most o' the horses are gone. Pa says to bring bandages an' medicine quick."

He went back to the scene of the fight with a heavy heart. Dead or dying horses lay in the bloody sand, with the bodies of half a dozen Indians among them. But it had been a costly victory for the white men. Only three of their own mounts remained alive, and two hunters had been put out of action. Now that the excitement was over, Jeff felt tired and listless. What hurt worst of all was the knowledge that his faithful buckskin would never carry him again.

chapter 18

LaCasse and Fitzpatrick held a council of war that afternoon. The wounded men had been carried to the boats and made as comfortable as possible. With only three horses left, it would be dangerous for the hunting party to stay on shore, at least as long as they were in Pawnee country, so it was decided that all would travel by river. By shifting some of the cargo, they made space for the ponies in the second boat. Then, with a favoring wind blowing from the west, they hoisted sail and shoved out into the Platte.

Jeff and his father were in the first boat, commanded by LaCasse. The burgeway ordered his Frenchmen to man the oars and took his place in the bow, stocky legs planted wide, holding a long hickory pole in his hands. He knew the river better, perhaps, than any man alive. Yet the current was constantly changing course and forming new bars where none had been before. LaCasse's practiced eye searched the fast-flowing brown water and his pole tested the bottom for unseen shoals.

The banks slipped past with deceptive speed. Actually, Jeff figured, they must be making close to ten miles an hour, aided by sail, current, and oars. That was faster than men on horseback could travel for any distance over a few miles.

And if they could keep it up hour after hour, he knew they would leave the Pawnee war party a long way behind.

At first he enjoyed the luxury of sitting grandly on the afterdeck and watching the prairie go by. Then the inactivity began to bore him. There was an interesting change when, in spite of LaCasse's watchfulness, the boat grated to a stop on a sandbar. It happened in the gathering dusk, soon after sunset.

Shouting strange French oaths, the burgeway ordered his men to take the sail down, ship oars, and man the poles. Jeff sprang to help and was soon straining away at his pole with the rest. They braced their legs and heaved till the sweat poured off them. And at last the boat worked free of the bar. The other craft, meanwhile, had swept past, her crew laughing and offering sarcastic advice. It was a full hour before they overtook her.

The sails were not hoisted again, but the boats kept on at a slower pace all night. A half-moon gave them enough light for drifting. Jeff slept soundly until he was wakened in the dawn mist by another grinding jolt. This time both boats had gone aground in shoal water close to the left bank, where the river made a bend to the right. And since poling would be of no help, Jeff was initiated into the mysteries of the *cordelle*.

Growling and stumbling, the sleepy boatmen went over the side into hip-deep water. A long, heavy rope, with one end made fast to the foot of the mast, was carried back upstream. When it was taut, all hands began to pull. They heaved with might and main, then eased up and hauled again to the steady rhythm of a French river song. Jeff, on the line with the others, felt the push of the current around his thighs and the washing out of mud under his feet. Once or twice he slipped, for it was hard to get a purchase on the soft, shifting bottom.

The crew strained and grunted for a long ten minutes

before the keel was freed from the shoal. Then they had to pull the boat off into deeper water, and a few held her there till the rest could get aboard and man the poles.

At sunrise the voyage was resumed. Nothing was said about breakfast, and Jeff was beginning to feel pretty hungry. His father gave him a piece of dried buffalo meat out of his "possible" sack, and he chewed on that for the next half hour. Then, as the mist cleared away, they could see rolling hills off to the south, and the green of trees along the riverside.

"Good place to land an' cook some food," LaCasse called. "You, Jacques—*à droit*—steer to the right!"

The bank was steeper and higher here, with enough water to pull the boats in close beneath the overhanging cottonwoods. They tied up and went ashore to find dry wood for a fire. Soon there was buffalo meat sizzling on spits over the flames and a good smell of coffee from the pots.

While the food was cooking, Fitzpatrick, John Barlow, and Jeff carried their rifles to the top of the low bluff for a look around. To the south and west the folds of prairie stretched empty. If the Pawnees had followed them, they had either been outdistanced or were well hidden.

"This child," said Fitz, "is goin' to feel better when we've put another day betwixt us."

Barlow nodded his agreement. "I reckon LaCasse knows it, too," he answered. "We'll be on our way as soon as those boatmen have filled their bellies. What do you make o' the weather?"

Fitzpatrick looked back to the west. "Goin' to be tarnation hot," he said. "Air feels heavy, too. That haze could build up into storm clouds 'fore the day's over."

The three went down the bluff again, ate their breakfast, and returned to the boats. Within an hour after they had come ashore, everyone was aboard and the moorings were cast off. There was hardly a breath of breeze that morning, and the sweating Frenchmen were ordered to the oars. By the time the sun stood overhead, the heat was stifling on the river.

Jeff stripped himself to the waist and lay on his blanket, napping or watching the hawks that wheeled lazily, high in the blue. The suffocating air made him sorry for the rowers. After a while the sun was obscured by haze, and when he looked astern, he saw that the whole western sky was a black mass of cloud.

LaCasse had seen it coming. Now he ordered the man at the sweep oar to steer for the shelter of a wooded island, half a mile downstream. The boats nosed in on a little sandbar that stretched from the foot of the island.

"Big wind, she's goin' to blow," the burgeway told his boatmen. "Tie down those tarpaulins—*vite!*"

They sprang to it, double-lashing the canvas covers over the bales of fur, and casting frightened glances at the sky as they worked. The boats were beached thirty or forty yards below the trees, but mooring lines were run upstream to the trunks of a couple of big cottonwoods. It was hardly done when the storm was on them.

Jeff had seen plenty of thunderstorms but never one like this. All the sky except a ragged streak to the eastward was as black as night. Out of it came an ominous, rumbling roar that mounted steadily in volume. And yet the air hung heavy and still.

With terrifying suddenness the lightning began to rip the black curtain overhead. It flashed downward in jagged streaks, followed instantly by deafening crashes of sound. Then came the wind.

"Lie down!" Jeff's father yelled. "Lie down and hang on!"

The boy obeyed, but even as he flung himself flat on the deck, he caught a glimpse of something that chilled his blood. Coming down the river from the southwest was a slim funnel of cloud, blacker even than the darkness around it.

The tornado hit the upper end of the island, ripping up trees by the roots, whirling them past overhead. Then by some fluke of nature the twister veered a little to the north. Its fiercely spinning vortex passed a hundred yards from the boats, though the winds around it blew with almost stunning force.

Jeff felt himself tossed from the deck as if by the sweep of a giant paw. The next moment he was floundering in water up to his armpits—water already churned to foaming waves. Four or five struggling Frenchmen were around him, all trying to claw their way back to the vessel. But the

boats were no longer on the sandbar. Wind and waves had driven them free.

The boy saw one of them looming dark a few feet away. He thrust up his arm in a desperate effort to gain a handhold, but his fingers slipped along the wet planking as it passed. Then, when he thought his last chance was gone, his wrist was seized in a powerful grip. His father, leaning down from the gunwale, hauled him up the side and aboard.

"There's some more men," Jeff panted. "Back there in the river."

"I know," John Barlow replied. "We'll get 'em."

He grabbed a pole as he spoke and helped the remaining members of the crew swing the boat around. The wind had

died as suddenly as it came. Within five minutes all the boatmen but one had been pulled out, choking and dripping.

"Where's Pierre?" the grim-faced LaCasse asked his crew.

They shook their heads. Nobody remembered seeing him in the wild moments after the twister struck. The air had been full of flying branches and debris, and those who had been thrown into the water were blindly trying to save themselves. Now that the storm was past, the two boats spent an hour poling along the shore, looking for the lost Pierre. At last the burgeway gave it up.

"A good riverman," he said sadly. "But he's gone for sure, and we can't wait any longer."

In the number two boat the horses had come through the storm safely, though they still trembled with fear. And the cargoes of beaver had suffered almost no damage.

"Could ha' been plenty worse," Fitzpatrick said. "If'n that thing hadn't swung off when it did, thar wouldn't ha' been many of us left."

Navigation was difficult during the few hours of daylight that remained. Hundreds of limbs and whole trees littered the river, piling up on the shoals and forming dams around which the water swirled in a brown, ugly torrent.

It was on one of these log jams, nearly a dozen miles downstream, that they found Pierre's body. It was crushed and battered and a huge splinter, torn from a tree, had been driven clear through his chest. When they tied up that evening, LaCasse once more read a simple funeral service and the man was buried among the cottonwoods.

* * * *

Five days later they reached the Missouri. To offset the drifted barriers that blocked the Platte in many places, they had the help of high water. A lot of rain must have fallen in the valley above them. It came boiling down out of the sandhill country with a force that sometimes spun the keelboats end for end and out of control.

There was constant work for the men at the poles and oars, and Jeff did his share, along with the other hunters. By the time they emerged into the big river the blisters on his hands had turned to calluses. He no longer thought of a keelboat voyage as a romantic adventure. It was hard, dangerous labor.

Most of their buffalo meat had spoiled in the heat before they came to the Missouri. Now, with the vengeful Pawnees left well behind, the mountain men took turns foraging for game. The day after they passed Council Bluffs, Jeff and his father saddled two of the ponies, led the third, and started off on a hunt while the Frenchmen were still at breakfast. They climbed the bluffs and rode along the eastern side of the Missouri.

It was a fine, clear morning, with meadowlarks singing in the prairie grass. The boy was happy just to be in the saddle again. But for a while it looked as if game would be hard to find. Though they ranged back as much as three miles from the river, they saw nothing bigger than a few prairie chickens. Jeff shot one of the birds, and they roasted it over a small fire for their midday meal. Then they pushed on southward, for John Barlow didn't want to fall too far behind the boats.

Late in the afternoon they were still some miles above the agreed mooring place. Ahead they could see the tops of trees in a draw that angled toward the river.

"Might as well follow it down," said Jeff's father. "There could be a deer or two in that brush along the bottom."

They rode quietly down the sandy bank beside the little stream, Jeff in the lead. Suddenly he saw something that made him pull the pony to a halt. In the mud just ahead were tracks—buffalo tracks! He pointed them out to his father, who rode up and nodded in agreement.

"Seem to be headed for the river," he murmured. "Or they could be down in those cottonwoods, keeping cool in the shade."

Jeff made sure his rifle was loaded and capped. Then he followed his father's cautious advance. After two or three hundred yards they both dismounted and tethered the ponies.

"Wind's from the west," John Barlow whispered. "But they can smell horses a long way off. Go low and quiet!"

Crouching and keeping to the cover of the trees, they moved on a short distance before Barlow stopped again. He pointed down the draw. Looking past his shoulder, Jeff saw a huge dark shape moving in the thicket. It was a big bull and he acted uneasy.

The range was still too great for accurate shooting, so the two hunters crawled patiently forward. At last they were within about fifty yards of the little herd. Jeff could count five other buffalo—cows and calves—all partially hidden by the foliage.

"Pick a good fat cow," John Barlow breathed. "I'll take the big one."

Even before he cocked his rifle, Jeff saw the bull toss his great head suspiciously. At the click all the animals started to move, but in so doing they came into clearer view. A plump young cow turned, coming into line with the boy's sights, and he squeezed the trigger at the same instant his father fired.

The bull fell in his tracks, but the cow was only wounded. With a choking bellow she went lumbering off down the draw in the wake of the others.

"Get your horse and follow her," Barlow ordered. "I'll stay and skin out the bull."

Jeff hurried back to the ponies, reloading the rifle as he ran. In a minute or two he was mounted and galloping downstream in pursuit. Through the trees he could see the lower end of the ravine, where it opened on the riverbank. The other two cows and their calves had already climbed the steep side of the draw and disappeared. The one he had shot made a valiant effort to follow them. He saw her struggle up the slope, slip to her knees, and fall back. Hating himself for his clumsiness in not killing her at the first shot, he rode up within a few paces and put a merciful bullet through her heart.

LaCasse, aboard the leading boat, must have been near enough to hear his shot, for before Jeff turned back to help his father, he saw both craft heading in to land at the mouth of the stream.

"Tie up!" he called cheerfully. "We've got a lot o' meat to bring aboard!"

chapter 19

There was enough fresh buffalo meat to last them all the way down to Independence. There, at the trading post, they were able to buy enough provisions to finish the voyage, so there was no more need to hunt.

They pulled into the company's dock at St. Louis eight days later. It had been early spring when they came over the South Pass. Now it was mid-July, and the corn was high in the fields they passed above the city.

While LaCasse supervised the unloading of the beaver, Fitzpatrick and the two Barlows checked in with their belongings at the Laramie House. Then they set out to pay their respects to General Ashley.

Jeff had given very little thought to how he looked in the past year. Now, as he walked past stores and fine houses, he realized that the conventionally clad citizens of St. Louis were casting amused glances in his direction. Suddenly he was conscious of his appearance.

He halted a moment in front of a shop window and looked at his reflection in the glass. What he saw there was a lanky six-foot scarecrow in tattered buckskins that were black with smoke and grease. The lean face was tanned as dark as an Indian's, and the long black hair, caught behind by a thong of deer hide, added to the savage impression.

Hastily he caught up with his companions and touched his father's arm. "Pa," he said, "I don't reckon I look fit to go in the General's house. Maybe I'd better spend a few o' my beaver on some city clothes."

Fitz threw back his head and laughed. "Don't fret about it, hoss!" he said. "Gin'ral Ashley's used to seein' mountain men, an' you got no call to be ashamed o' bein' one."

They came to a street of fine residences and went up the steps to the door of one of the largest. A moment later a Negro manservant had ushered them into the hall. It was the first real mansion Jeff had ever entered. At the door of the study stood a tall, imposing-looking man, smiling a greeting. He was handsomely dressed in a long, high-collared coat and strapped pantaloons. White linen ruffles showed at his throat, and graying hair swept upward above his aristocratic face.

"So it's you, Fitz!" he exclaimed cordially. "Back from a good season, they tell me. John Barlow, too. And this must be your son. The resemblance is amazing. Where's that partner of yours, John—the old fellow who used to trap the Wind River country?"

"I'm sorry, sir," said Jeff's father. "I thought you might have heard. He died from a Cheyenne arrow, and we buried him in the South Pass."

They went on to tell of Slim's passing. "He sort o' made the boy, here, his heir," Fitzpatrick explained. "Left him all his beaver, so he kin go east an' l'arn to be a painter. Not that he's got much l'arnin' to do, fur's I kin see. Ye'd ought to take a look at some of his picters, Gin'ral."

The head of the Rocky Mountain Fur Company directed his keen glance at Jeff while the boy fidgeted uneasily.

"I'd like to see them," he said. "Could you bring them here tomorrow?"

"Yes, sir," Jeff mumbled. "I'd be proud to."

* * * *

It was a different-looking young man who knocked at the door next day. Jeff had had a hot bath and a haircut, and been fitted out in a decent white shirt and a coat and trousers. He even wore new boots, on feet that were used to the soft comfort of moccasins. As a consequence, he walked a bit stiffly as he was shown into General Ashley's study.

The older man looked up from his desk and smiled. "You're as good as your word, I see," he remarked. "And the paintings—are those what you're carrying?"

"Yes, sir. They've come through a couple of Indian fights an' the ford o' the Platte an' even a tornado, but I guess they're still whole."

He unrolled the soft deerskin bundle and spread nine pictures on the floor. The General had risen to his feet. Now he bent over to look more closely.

"By George!" he exclaimed. "The Red Buttes! I'd know them anywhere. And this one of the buffalo hunt—that's a Crow warrior, I'll be bound!"

"Yes, sir. That's Running Wolf. He's a son of old White Calf. I tried to draw White Calf's face in this picture here."

There was more than mere politeness in Ashley's enthusiasm. "They're excellent!" he cried. "Other artists have tried to paint the West, and none have come very close. But these have motion and action! How did you ever get such effects when you had only red and black paint?"

Embarrassed, Jeff tried to tell him. "You'll never know, General, how I used to wish for a whole raft o' colors. But trade vermilion an' charcoal were all I had handy, so I did the best I could. I'm mighty pleased you like 'em."

"Like them!" Ashley said. "I've got to have these for my walls! Reminders of the years I've spent in the Rockies—the scenery and the game and the mountain men! I've no idea what they're worth, but I'll give you five hundred dollars for the lot."

Jeff stood there stunned, unable to speak a word.

"If you don't think that's enough," said the General, "I'll be glad to match anybody else's offer."

"Oh, it—it isn't that, sir," Jeff stammered hastily. "I was just—well—sort o' knocked over by the idea anyone would pay that kind o' money. Why, that's more than eighty plew!"

Ashley's head went back in a roar of laughter. "You *are* a mountain man, sure enough!" he exclaimed. "Some people might want to frame these, but I like them just as they are—on deerskin. It's a fine idea—your going east to study. Some day I expect you'll be coming back a famous artist."

He counted out the money in crisp banknotes. As Jeff put them in his pocket, the General gave him a fatherly pat on the shoulder.

"Young man," he said, "you're making your move at the right time. You've seen that country out there—the finest country in the world—while it was new and fresh. I'm afraid it will never be quite the same again. I'll tell you something I wouldn't tell Fitz or the other old-timers for fear it would break their hearts. The price of beaver's due to go down! Word came last week that some of the London hatters are planning to use silk instead of beaver for top hats. Of course, it won't happen all at once, but I'm afraid it means the end of high-priced fur."

He shook his head sadly. "That won't affect me too much," he went on, "for I've made a comfortable fortune.

But I hate to think of the old trappers and what it will do to them."

Jeff, too, felt distressed. "My father," he said, "figures there'll be a lot o' folks moving out to Oregon soon. Maybe some o' the mountain men can get jobs guiding the wagon trains and supplying 'em with meat."

Ashley nodded. "That's occurred to me, too," he said. "Perhaps I can help to arrange it when the time comes. Good luck to you, my boy!"

Jeff shook hands once more and went down the steps feeling more grown up than ever before in his life. Not only did he have money—a lot of money—that he had earned himself, but he was the friend and confidant of one of the most famous men in St. Louis!

Back at the hotel he showed the banknotes to his father. Usually a quiet man, John Barlow was astounded when he heard what Ashley had paid for the paintings.

"That'll be a big help, Jeffy!" he exclaimed. "I only hope the General really thought they were worth it. We wouldn't want him to be cheated."

"I know," Jeff answered. "I'd have thought fifteen or twenty dollars apiece was plenty, but he really did want 'em, an' he seemed to think this was a fair price."

The next day they cashed in their fur and put the money in a local bank. When the time came to start for the East, they could carry the necessary traveling funds and take a bank draft along to cover their living expenses after their arrival.

"I figure the place we want to head for is Philadelphia," John Barlow told his son. "Some o' the best artists in the country studied there. Gilbert Stuart and Benjamin West and the Peales. Nowadays they've got the Pennsylvania Academy of the Fine Arts. If you're good enough to get in at the Academy, I reckon they'll teach you all you want to know. Meantime, I aim to go back into teaching if I can find a school there. I used to be a pretty fair country teacher."

The next steamboat heading for the Ohio River and Pittsburgh wouldn't be leaving until the following week. Jeff used the time to purchase canvas, brushes, and a dozen tubes of precious oil paint. He chose the colors carefully, knowing just how he wanted to use them.

Most of the preliminary sketches he had made in their winter camp had been preserved, and now he set to work to translate one of them into color. It was a frustrating job. He found there was a great deal he needed to learn about mixing colors and laying them on the canvas. It seemed to him his picture lost the freshness he had captured when working with his homemade tools and paints.

Discouraged, he threw his palette aside when the light began to fail and went downstairs to join his father for supper.

"What's the matter, son?" John Barlow asked him. "Your face looks as long as your arm."

"I just can't seem to catch it," Jeff answered gloomily. "Looks like I'll never make a painter."

His father hid his smile and tried to look sympathetic. "Been at it all of half a day, haven't you?" he said. "Maybe that's too soon to decide. It's been my experience that most worthwhile things don't come easy. Let's forget it for a bit and get something to eat."

They were on their way into the hotel dining room when they heard a voice behind them.

"Mist' Barlow, suh?"

Jeff looked over his shoulder and recognized the speaker. "It's General Ashley's man, Pa," he murmured.

The Negro was bowing politely. "The General requests your presence at dinner, suh," he said in a soft, melodious voice. "And the young gentleman, too—most particular.

The carriage is outside, suh, if you'll be so good as to come with me."

"Thanks," John Barlow told him. "It's a bit unexpected, so maybe you'd better give us a few minutes to dress up."

Somewhat mystified by the sudden invitation, they hustled into their best clothes and were soon rolling through the streets behind a matched pair of grays. At the Ashley mansion they were shown directly to the study. The General was a courtly figure as he rose to greet them.

"I asked you both here," he said, "to meet a friend of mine from New Orleans. This is Monsieur Duval—John Barlow, Jefferson Barlow. Be seated, gentlemen. Dinner will be served shortly."

Monsieur Duval was a plump little man with spectacles, spiky mustaches, and a neatly trimmed goatee. His eyes twinkled merrily behind his glasses as he bowed and smiled.

"I believe," said General Ashley, "you were planning to start for the East in a few days to give the boy a chance for training in the field of art. Perhaps there's a different solution. Monsieur Duval is a well-known painter. His portraits, landscapes, and animal studies have been exhibited in Paris as well as in America. He has been considering making his home in St. Louis and would like to start a little school of painting if he can find young artists of ability."

He turned toward Jeff then with a smile. "I—er—took the liberty of showing him your Rocky Mountain pictures," he said.

The Frenchman made an eager gesture. *"Mais oui!"* he exclaimed. *"Ils sont superbes!* I do not speak well ze English—but you draw ver' good, Monsieur! Ze 'orse—ze buffalo—*et les sauvages! Tous sont magnifiques!"*

The only French Jeff knew was some of the *patois* he had picked up from the keelboatmen. But he understood the drift of Duval's remarks and reddened under his tan.

At that point they were called in to dinner, and he sat down to such a repast as he had never seen. It began with a clear soup, followed by broiled trout, roast prairie chicken, sirloin of beef, and a well-seasoned salad. Finally came raspberry tarts with whipped cream and thick black New Orleans coffee. The finest of French wines were served throughout the meal. Then, over brandy and cigars, the men discussed Jeff's future.

"St. Louis," General Ashley told them "will soon be the metropolis of the West, rivaling New York and Philadelphia in trade and culture. It's the gateway to the whole vast territory of the Missouri, the Rockies, and the Pacific Coast. As a citizen of St. Louis, I take a natural pride in its advancement and would like to see it become a center of the arts. Quite simply, John, if you and your son would agree to stay here, I'd be happy to pay for the cost of his instruction under Monsieur Duval."

The words caught Jeff and his father by surprise. For half a minute John Barlow sat silent, puffing on his cigar. Then he looked up with a grin.

"That's a mighty generous offer, General," he said. "I don't want to sound ungrateful, but I'd have to say no to the last part of it. You see, we're mountain men, Jeff and I. We're used to standing on our own feet, and if we decide to stay here, I reckon we can pay Monsieur Duval out o' what we've laid by. Maybe we'd better take a day or so to think it over."

"Fair enough," said Ashley with a laugh. "I know how independent you mountain men are, so I rather expected such an answer. But the offer still stands if you need it."

Their parting was cordial, and Jeff and his father walked slowly back to the hotel through the hot summer night.

"What do you think, Pa?" the boy asked. "Far's I'm concerned, it makes a lot o' sense. I reckon this Frenchman knows his business, an' think o' the money we'd save if we didn't have to travel all the way to Philadelphia!"

Barlow smiled. "That part's no bother," he said. "But I'm glad you like Duval. I'll look around tomorrow and see if I can get myself a job. Maybe the best plan'll be to try it for a few months. Then, if you don't think you're learning all you should, we can always head east."

* * * *

A week later the Ohio River steamboat left without them. They had moved from the hotel to the upper floor of a modest house on the Rue de l'Eglise. It had a big attic room with a skylight facing north, where Jeff could paint to his heart's content. After a couple of lessons with Duval he knew he was beginning to get the kind of instruction he needed. Their language difficulties were unimportant, for Jeff studied the Frenchman's color techniques and learned quickly how to handle his brush strokes.

John Barlow, meanwhile, was back in his old profession, happy to be teaching in one of the city's best schools.

"We're set for a while, anyhow," he told Jeff. "Any time we get restless, o' course, we can pack up our possibles and light out for that valley o' Slim's. I reckon there'll still be a few beaver there, and a buffalo or two to eat on the way."

Jeff grinned with understanding. "You talk that way an' you'll make us both restless," he said. "But I've set out to learn to paint—remember? So let's forget about the mountains for a while. When I know I'm ready, there's a lot o' things up there I want to put on canvas. Right now all I can do is dream about it—and keep my powder dry and my rifle oiled!"

He went back to his garret studio and worked as long as the light lasted. Then he left his easel and turned to the little dormer window that looked out over the rooftops to the west. The view was dreary enough. But when he closed his eyes, he could see again the great white peaks, fading to pink and purple in the sunset.

Someday, he knew, he would go back.

www.ingramcontent.com/pod-product-compliance
Lightning Source LLC
Chambersburg PA
CBHW060600190726
48283CB00003B/1100

* 9 7 8 1 9 3 1 1 7 7 1 9 1 *